THE FENOKEE PROJECT

Everything was going well for Ben South and his partner. With the signed contract for the Cornelius hotel chain in their pocket, their future as building contractors looked bright. Then a letter arrived from Canada and overnight everything changed. Seven years earlier, South's young wife had died in Canada when her car skidded on a lonely road. The verdict was accidental death, but South now has reason to wonder: was it murder? He travels to Canada where he tangles with tycoon Grant Starling and his Fenokee Project – and realizes he is up against something much bigger than a single murder...

THE FENOKEE PROJECT

THE FENOKEE PROJECT

by

Roy Lewis

Dales Large Print Books
Long Preston, North Yorkshire,
BD23 4ND, England.

British Library Cataloguing in Publication Data.

Lewis, Roy
    The Fenokee project.

    A catalogue record of this book is
    available from the British Library

    ISBN   978-1-84262-602-3 pbk

First published in Great Britain 1971
by William Collins Sons & Co. Ltd.

Copyright © Roy Lewis 1971

Cover illustration © Arcangel

Published in Large Print 2008 by arrangement with
Mr Roy Lewis

Dales Large Print is an imprint of Library Magna Books Ltd.

Printed and bound in Great Britain by
T.J. (International) Ltd., Cornwall, PL28 8RW

CHAPTER 1

1

P.R Cornelius put his fingertips together, pursed his lips and gazed thoughtfully at the ceiling.

'I'll be frank with you, gentlemen.'

Ben South glanced at Pete Henley and grimaced. In his experience when a man said he'd be frank he was about to be just the opposite. Pete's face was expressionless, the heavy brow smooth, the eyes calm.

'I've now had the opportunity to go through your tenders completely,' Cornelius continued. 'I've checked on every costing item and I'm pleased to say you've done a very thorough job. The Hotels Chain is a very complicated piece of business and there's a lot of money involved but you've gone into it all thoroughly, most thoroughly.'

Cornelius paused, and one pink hand stole up to smooth his bald head.

'Nevertheless, there's just one thing that bothers me.'

Here it comes, Ben thought to himself, the pay-off. He looked down, staring at his hands. He wanted this contract, it was the breakthrough for Henley and South, and he'd put a lot of work into those tenders.

'Now let me recap,' Cornelius was saying in that reedy voice. 'You, Mr South, are mainly responsible for the figures. I understand you came to England from Canada, where you were a qualified surveyor.'

'That's right. Six years ago.' And met a dissatisfied architect called Pete Henley, Ben thought to himself.

'You and Mr Henley set up in partnership, formed a building company and it would seem you've done quite well ... in a small way.'

'We've been successful,' Pete said quietly. A small line had appeared between his bushy eyebrows.

'Quite. But you'll appreciate my situation. I don't wish to question your capabilities, gentlemen, but in tendering for the Hotels Chain, couldn't one say you're ... ah ... biting off more than you can chew?'

'We don't think so,' Ben said. 'You've seen our figures; they're solid figures and I'm convinced that–'

'I'm not questioning your figures, Mr South, but your experience. Let me put it this way. You're a building firm that has made a reputation for itself in the industrial field. There are two major directors – yourself, and Mr Henley. Your finance is limited, your opportunities for expansion to meet crises minimal. I'm more than a little worried that you might not be able to honour your commitments should the contract be given to you.'

Ben leaned forward and injected as much earnestness into his tone as he could raise.

'Mr Cornelius, we can swing it. You've already seen my costing. Within those figures I've included the hiring charges for machinery and earthmoving equipment that we don't own. I've got other documents back at the office which'll show you how we've sorted out efficient labour sub-contracts. All contingencies have been covered. I am more than confident–'

'Young men are always confident,' Cornelius replied, and rubbed his fingertips together a little more quickly. 'I've already told you how impressed I am by your tenders and your working plans, but to be frank, I'm reluctant to advise my board that we should take a chance with such a young firm. I ... ah ... like your style, gentlemen, but I'm not certain that you have the backing to carry it through.'

Ben looked quickly towards Pete, but his partner was still remaining cool. Ben fished in his briefcase and pulled out a sheet of paper. He handed it to Cornelius.

'What we lack in backing we make up in energy and application,' he said. 'That's a list of our current commitments. You'll notice how wide and diverse they are.'

Silence fell, broken only by Cornelius drumming spasmodically on the polished desk surface with his left hand as he read through the list of contracts Ben had given him.

'Impressive,' he said at last, then rose and stood in front of the window, staring out to the busy street. Behind his back his pink hands clenched and unclenched. Abruptly he turned to face Ben and Pete.

'All right. I'll take a chance.'

'You'll accept our tenders?'

'Once they've been through our tendering department for a final check, I'll recommend to the board that you be given the contract for the first three hotels. Thereafter, we'll proceed again.'

'Mr Cornelius–' Ben began in excitement, but the little man raised a pink hand.

'There are conditions, Mr South. First – I've seen your list of present commitments, and I am impressed by them, but I also fear that such a programme may well interfere with the successful completion of your contracts with Cornelius Ltd, so I must be assured on this point. If you take the contract with us, you must accept no other contractual bids.'

Ben hesitated. He was aware of Pete moving uncertainly in his chair.

'There's another condition?'

'Yes. I'm still not convinced you could undertake a project of this size as you stand. The second condition is that you take in new capital, expand your working capital and constitute a larger and financially more stable board of directors. The obvious man to join your board would be Sir John Emsley. With his experience of the industry and the financial injection he could give your company your battle would be half won. Naturally he'd expect some measure of financial control. He would also be able to name two or three other people who could join your board in addition. In such a situation, I feel sure my board would approve the acceptance of your tenders for the Hotels Chain.'

Cornelius sat down abruptly, placed his fingertips together once more and contemplated them.

'This'll take thinking about,' Ben said slowly.

'I'm afraid I'd require a decision from you within two days, Mr South. If you decide to accept the contract and its conditions, naturally you'd have six months or more within which to implement them. But time presses, and there are other tenders...'

'We'll think about it,' Pete Henley said and rose to his feet. Cornelius pressed a buzzer on his desk and moments later a girl came in to show the two partners out of the office.

Cornelius shook hands with them cordially enough but his grip was soft and flabby.

'I don't like that feller,' Pete Henley said as they walked out to the street in front of the Cornelius Building and hailed a cab. He said nothing more until they reached the offices of Henley and South, across the other side of town.

Then, in the confines of his own office, he swore, reached for the bottle of whisky that he kept in the second drawer of his desk and poured two drinks. He handed one to Ben.

'To the contract that never was.'

'How do you mean?'

'Hell, Ben, you're not thinking of taking up the Cornelius contract?'

Ben put down his glass and stared at his partner. Pete was shorter than he was, built like an overweight Teddy-bear, but he had a temper that needed watching and he seemed on the point of exploding now.

'It's our chance to make the big time,' Ben said quietly. 'I don't see how we can afford to turn down the offer.'

'I don't see how we can afford to take it!' Pete scratched vigorously and desperately at his thatch of black hair. 'You can't suggest that we're going to accept the conditions Cornelius laid down.'

'But they're sensible from his point of view, and they give us entry to a big contract. Moreover, he's right when he says we need more financial backing, and a reconstituted board would–'

'Aw, grow up, Ben! Can't you see what Cornelius is up to? He sees our tenders, knows they're good – so he accepts them, on condition he gets a slice of the cake. You must know that Emsley is one of his own directors. If Emsley and the other two nominees join us we'll be half owned by Cornelius. And the hint Cornelius dropped about Emsley having a measure of financial control just shows how much say we'd have in anything. It's a non-starter, Ben.'

'I can't agree.' Ben watched his partner bridle, saw his face darken, but firmly he went on. 'We're a small firm, but we're a good one. We've got something to offer Cornelius, so we don't just cave in on a new board. We'll stipulate that the new members nominated take no more than a twenty per cent slice, and that Emsley be made only Joint Financial Director. That way we'll ensure that control of the undertaking stays firmly in our hands.'

Pete shook his head in disagreement.

'I just don't like it, Ben. Even if they agreed to that arrangement–'

'They'd have to or there's no go.'

'–there's still the matter of the other commitments. Hell, Ben, Cornelius is asking us to lay off tendering for other contracts so that we would concentrate entirely on his Hotels Chain project. What happens if that goes up in the air? What if something went wrong? We'd be left high and dry.'

'Credit me with more sense. If we go into this thing we'll have to reach agreement on a compensation clause written into the contract, so that if any breach occurs adequate compensation will be paid. The hiring charges for equipment, for instance, they could cripple us if we didn't watch out for that, but believe me, Pete, I'm not going into this with my eyes closed.'

Pete Henley sat down behind his desk and placed one massive foot upon the desk top. He sipped at his whisky, eyeing Ben over the rim of the glass. He drew his heavy brows together.

'You want this Cornelius contract badly.'

'I think *we* need it, Pete.'

'You know I'm not convinced.'

'*I* am.'

Pete sighed, put down his glass and folded his arms. Slowly he shook his head in resignation.

'Okay. I don't like it, but I've a healthy respect for your business sense and your hunches. We've done well together, and maybe you're right that this is the way to hit the jackpot. I don't like it, Ben, but I'll go along with it. We'll do as Cornelius suggests.'

Ben grinned, drained his glass and leaned over to slap Pete on the shoulder.

'You won't regret it, Pete.'

Pete Henley regarded him with the world-weary look reserved by the middle-aged man who's been around for the young man pushing for the top.

'All I ask is, when we go broke, just allow me to say I told you so.'

2

During the next few days Pete dealt with the progress chasing on outstanding contracts leaving Ben to take the Cornelius matter further. Ben was able to arrange a meeting with Sir John Emsley, who expressed a willingness to join the board of Henley and South Ltd, and the company solicitors were informed of the impending agreements.

Everything seemed to be going well, and even Pete was warming to the idea. Then the letter arrived.

It was airmail, from Canada. Ben recognized the writing on it and the addressee's name on the reverse side confirmed his guess. It was from his father, John South.

Inside the envelope was another, crumpled, bearing Ben's name but with several addresses scribbled over. His father's accompanying note was brief.

'Ben – This finally arrived at my address. It

would seem to be for you. She must have got my address from the Fairmont police.'

The sender's name was unfamiliar: Mrs Ellen Pearl. The address – Waterton Park – meant nothing to him. Ben ripped open the crumpled envelope.

'Dear Mr South,

You won't know me and I reckon you won't appreciate that this is the most difficult letter I've ever had to write. But it's got to be done because I'm a God-fearing woman and brought up by my folks to believe that what's right is right, even if it hurts. I always thought Joe, my husband, was built that way too and it grieves me most now to think that he should have acted the way he did. I'm sorry in a way that he ever told me about it, because I can't rest easy on account of it, but I know he had to tell me because when you're facing your Maker you've got to make your peace. Joe's at peace now, but I can't live with what he told me, not live with it still inside me, shaming me because of what Joe did.

It's about your wife, Mr South. Joe did a wrong thing there and it was done out of sinful desire for gain and I wish I could give it all back but things haven't gone well with us these last two years and there's no chance of my being able to pay you back in any way

– other than in telling you what happened, and what he did.

Maybe it's not important, and I hope that it isn't but it was wrong and I'd esteem it a favour if you'd get in touch with me, so I can unburden myself more fully than is possible in this letter which may get into the hands of strangers.

I hope to hear from you soon.

Yrs sincerely,

Ellen Pearl.'

Ben read the letter three times and it still made little sense but he wasn't sure whether this was due to the guarded tone of the letter or to the fact that his mind was spinning violently with a succession of images arising before him.

He had thought it was all finished, he had thought he'd come out of the darkness but it was still there, hovering at the edges of his mind, blurring his senses with the pain of recall.

He glanced at his watch, folded the letter and returned it to its envelope. Pete was due in at the office in half an hour. Ben waited.

He waited dully, unable to think clearly. He needed to talk about this, needed to speak so that some semblance of order could emerge out of the chaos at present in his brain. He walked along to the washroom and splashed cold water on his face but he still felt muzzy; the earnest face that stared back at him from the mirror was his own, yet unfamiliar. The dark hair, the puzzled eyes, the square chin, the small scar on the cheekbone, they seemed to belong to a stranger, an English businessman, not the surveyor who had left Canada six years ago.

Six years.

He heard the door to Pete's room bang and Ben dried his hands and face quickly. He walked to Pete's room, tapped on the door and entered as Pete bellowed permission.

'Oh, it's you, Ben. I've just been down to the Kenry site – it looks as though we'll get that one finished well within schedule. And I signed those papers you gave me on the Cornelius contract last night but forgot to bring them into the office. I'm not–'

He broke off and eyed Ben, a suspicious bear snuffling over its cub.

'You all right?'

'I'm all right.'

'You don't look good. I'll get you a whisky. The only panacea.'

He pulled open the desk drawer but Ben forestalled him.

'I just received a letter, Pete.'

'So?'

Ben handed Pete the letter and the heavy brows frowned with concentration as he read it. Slowly he handed it back and in a puzzled tone said:

'What's that all about?'

'I don't know.' Abruptly Ben turned, closed the door and sat down in front of Pete's desk. The big man hesitated, then also sat down. 'We've not talked too much about Canada, have we, Pete?'

Henley shrugged his broad shoulders.

'We didn't need to. When we met I was impressed by the feller I saw, and the longer we been in business together the more I'm impressed. As an architect I was drifting nowhere; in this operation, well, I get along. Canada was never relevant.'

'I'm referring to my personal life.'

'That was even less relevant, Ben,' Pete said softly, and Ben was suddenly aware that the pain must have shown more than he'd realized in those early days. Pete had seen it, but had never asked about it.

'I ran from Canada,' Ben said simply.

'Ben–'

'No, I want to talk about it, Pete, and I want you to hear. We've been partners and good friends but I've never told you… You did ask me once if I was married. I told you my wife was dead. We never discussed it again.'

'That's right.'

Because Ben hadn't wanted to discuss it, that was the way it had been. He wanted to discuss it now.

'I was pretty young when I met her. Twenty-two. I'd been brought up in Canada though my parents were English – they emigrated to Canada when I was a kid. Dad wanted me to join him in his engineering business when I grew up but I kicked against that, as young men will. I ended up as a surveyor, and I was working on a building project in Toronto when I met Joanna.'

He hesitated. Pete looked away and fiddled for his pipe, began to tamp tobacco into its bowl as Ben went on.'

'It was a cold day, a high wind was blowing and she was walking along Bloor Street with a silly fur hat that framed her face... We got married just a year later. I had no money but my parents helped out and we got an apartment in the city while she worked as a secretary at a school in the suburbs. She was mighty pretty, Pete.'

Pete scratched a match on the chair-leg and lit his pipe. He said nothing; there was nothing to say.

'Things were fine for a year or more. Then I got a job working on the St Lawrence Seaway. It meant I was away from home a lot but that couldn't be helped. I think she understood. I know she did. Her old man lived about a hundred miles away and she went to see him pretty often. Once or twice she came up to the project to see me but most times I made the trip back every two weeks for a couple of days at a time. We were still doing the preliminary work on a new section at that time. Then her father died.'

Ben's hands were damp. It had been a long time since he'd cared to recall those days.

'I should have realized then that I ought to change my job, or get Joanna nearer to me, and we did talk for a while of bringing her to Cornwall where I'd get to see her more often. But we didn't get around to it, the contract I was working on would run out in six months and ... well, we didn't move. Then, when I got back, things were different.'

Pete's eyes were on him, brown and friendly and sympathetic. At one time Ben couldn't have taken sympathy.

'I can't explain how things were different. She was just ... well, not so dependent on me, I suppose. But I was young and it rankled a bit. We didn't get on too well for a while. Then I took this job in Alberta at Wabamun Lake and we got an apartment in Edmonton and I got home weekends. Things got better.

'She wasn't working then and time got heavy on her hands. She had an old schoolfriend from the East called Mary Davis who was living in Red Deer and she took to going down there on occasions, during the week, while I was away. I never met Mary though I spoke to her on the phone a few times. I should have gone to see her after Joanna died but I never did.'

'What happened?'

21

'To Joanna? I don't know exactly. No one does. I didn't get home that weekend; I phoned and told Joanna I couldn't make it because some work had come up and she said it didn't matter, she'd go down to see Mary. I felt she sounded kind of distant when she spoke to me but I put it down to her disappointment that we couldn't be together. I didn't ever see her again.'

The news had come to him at the site on the lake; he could remember even now the strained red face of the engineer who had told him. He could also remember the numbing shock.

'Not far from Red Deer,' Ben continued, 'there's a valley called Fairmont Valley. Joanna had been driving down the valley and she must have skidded, ploughed right off the side of the road and down among some trees. It was possible she wasn't seriously hurt, just dazed, for she got out of the car and tried to make it up to the road. The inquest ... the coroner hazarded a guess as to the rest. In her dazed condition she just didn't make it. She wandered maybe for an hour, maybe longer, then she just lay down in the snow. They didn't find her for two days.'

Pete drew thoughtfully on his pipe. Without looking at Ben he said:

'Didn't her friend worry about her?'

'She never made it to Mary's. It seems she hadn't rung through to say she was coming

22

so she wasn't expected. For that matter, no one knew why she was in Fairmont Valley either – she must have taken the wrong road or maybe the highway was blocked or something.'

'What did the police tell you about it?'

Ben stared at his hands.

'I didn't see the police.'

Pete said nothing; he was aware of the new strain that was showing in Ben's face, new, and yet old as six years.

'I didn't make enquiries. I told you, Pete, I ran from Canada. We've been friends for six years and you probably think you understand me. But do you really? I don't understand myself. I can no more account for my conduct out there at Wabamun than I can teach a dog to talk. When I got the news about Joanna I went to pieces. It was as though all the iron left me. I was good for nothing; I threw in my job, I wouldn't go see my parents, I wouldn't even look at Joanna to identify her. My father had to do that. I didn't want to *know*, you understand.'

'Yes,' Pete said softly. 'I think I do.'

'I didn't want to know she was dead because in a sense I'd been a contributory cause. If I hadn't been stuck on my work, if I hadn't been racing off to the sites all the time, if I'd put her before my job she wouldn't have gone visiting her friend, she wouldn't have ended up on that highway in the snow, on her hands and knees, crawling until she lay down and died of exposure.'

Pete shuffled uncomfortably in his chair. His teeth clamped on his pipe; he didn't know what to say.

'I don't see how you can blame yourself that way. Her death was an accident.'

'That's what the coroner said, but don't you see how I was blaming myself? All right, I look back now and maybe I see an element of masochism in my conduct, but the fact is I was torn up by her death and I wanted to get away from it, entirely. In the end, I did. By running.'

'You didn't go down to Fairmont Valley?'

'No. Later I got a letter from my father; he told me he'd gone to see the police at Fairmont and had the whole story, how she'd probably wandered in the valley from the main highway and got stuck there but I didn't want to know. Everything was finished for me in Canada. So I left, I didn't want to be reminded of her because it was just pain. So I came to England. I ran to a new life, a new job, a new environment.'

'And we got together and set up in business and here we are.'

'And here's this letter.'

'I don't understand that letter.'

'No more than I do. I've no idea who this Mrs Pearl might be. It's probably a lot of nonsense but she seems to be implying that she can tell me something about Joanna's death. I'm not sure.'

'You think it's cranky?'

'Hell, I don't know. But don't you sense something odd about it? I mean, it's got a sort of old-world air about it, don't you think?'

Pete hesitated before answering.

'It certainly has an air of … pain about it.'

'So what do I do, Pete?'

'Have that whisky, for a start.' Pete put down his pipe, got out the bottle and poured them each a drink. 'When you're in the office it costs me a packet,' he said. 'We drink more whisky…'

He tilted back in his chair and looked into the glass dreamily.

'Good scotch, this… What ever became of that Carol girl, Ben?'

'Carol?'

Pete's brown eyes remained fixed on the golden liquid in the glass as he said casually,

'Yes, Carol Taylor. You remember, you met her over at the Weston party that Christmas when Joe Weston got locked out at three in the morning.'

'Oh yes. Carol Taylor.'

'Harriet and I … we thought you two had something going, for a while.'

'It petered out.'

'Was it Joanna?'

Pete was looking at him now and his eyes

25

were frank. Ben shrugged despondently.

'Hell, I don't know, it was all of two years ago and a lot of water has gushed since then.'

Pete made no reply and after a moment Ben picked up his drink.

'Yes, all right, I guess it *was* Joanna. She … I liked Carol all right, and we got along fine, but it wasn't the same, Pete, there was something wrong about it–'

'It didn't look wrong.'

'No. But I was wrong. I wasn't seeing Carol, I was seeing, looking for Joanna.'

'Did you tell Carol?'

'How do you tell a girl a thing like that?'

Pete grunted non-committally, reached for the bottle and poured himself another drink. He saluted Ben with a wry grin.

'Well, that settles that, then.'

'What?'

'The letter.'

'You've lost me.'

'You go see about it. You fly to Canada. You chase up this Ellen Pearl character and you check what it's all about.'

'But I just can't chase off like that, Pete!'

'Who's going to miss you for a week or so? Don't try making out to me you're the indispensable one around here.'

'But there's the Kenry site, and the Cornelius papers and all the–'

Pete held up a big beefy hand and waved it until Ben stopped.

'Partner. Let's face facts. With that letter on your mind you wouldn't be able to concentrate on anything to do with the business.'

'That's crazy! Some crank writes me a letter and you think–'

'No.' Again Pete stopped him and his heavy face was serious and concerned. 'It's not that, Ben. It's six years saying nothing about Joanna, it's Carol Taylor, it's the look on your face when you came in here with that letter. It's what's eating you up, feller. I can handle things back here for ten days or so. But if you don't cut out now and take off for Canada you'll spend the *next* six years wondering whether you should have gone or not. If you ask me, it's time you got the whole thing out of your system.'

He was right, of course. Ben's feelings and motives were mixed, confused by his inability to put into true perspective the part that Joanna had played in his life, the part that she was still playing now. But Pete was right; there was only one answer to the problem. Canada.

He had to meet Mrs Pearl, talk to her, listen to whatever she had to say – and at the same time eradicate from inside him all the scars that had been left by a cold afternoon in Fairmont Valley, seven years ago.

Ben returned to his flat that evening and he read and re-read Ellen Pearl's letter. He drafted a cable to her for transmission next morning and he made an Air Canada reservation through to Vancouver for the beginning of the next week. He returned to the letter and puzzled about its contents. 'Sinful desire for gain.' He repeated the words aloud. They had almost an Old Testament ring about them – but what would they have to do with Joanna's death in the snow seven years ago?

Seven years.

A long time. Ben South was a different man with a different life. Yet he couldn't have changed, not that much, not if the thought of Canada and of Joanna could turn him upside down this way.

He had thought it all dead and gone, but it wasn't.

CHAPTER 2

1

It was five years since Ben South had seen his father so it was natural that he should first call on him at his home near Vancouver. It was a strangely unsatisfactory meeting; they had never been close, and their corresponding had been intermittent since Ben's mother had died. John South had retired a year earlier and moved into the suburbs to a small, unpretentious house, and seemed to be enjoying life. Yet he seemed constrained by his son's company, particularly in view of the errand which had brought him back to Canada.

He was unable to shed any light on the situation. He reminded Ben rather coolly of the fact that when Joanna died it had had to be John South who flew to Red Deer to view the body, sort out the funeral arrangements, and make enquiries as to the accident. He made no outspoken criticism of his son's collapse at that time, but it lay in his attitude nevertheless, like a sword edge concealed in velvet. He told Ben that he had called on the police and attended the inquest, and that there had been a straightforward verdict of accidental death. The police had been a little puzzled as to why she had been in Fairmont Valley but they were not concerned to enquire deeply; it was quite probable she had taken the wrong turning at Valley Fork and proceeded up to Fairmont rather than on to Red Deer. The weather had been bad; it had been snowing heavily that morning.

Ben was not unhappy to take leave of the old man. He felt a momentary pang at the realization that this should have been a pleasurable occasion, a reunion of father and son, but he thrust the thought to the back of his mind. He had to go to see Ellen Pearl. John South had never heard of her or her husband.

He reached Waterton Park late the next evening. Ben had never been to the Waterton-Glacier International Peace Park before; he drove his rented car through the winding valleys and past the lakes with an eye on the immense wilderness about him, sky-cradled, cloud-banked mountains and forests, wide lakes and rivers. The park had been established in 1932 as a symbol of goodwill between Canada and the United States and he found himself presented with a breathtaking view as he skirted the grey escarpment and took the road that wound around the northern limits of Waterton's chain of lakes. Waterton Park turned out to be a quiet, dead-end village, a sojourn for relatively wealthy retired people.

Ben booked in at a motel on the edge of Waterton Lake and took dinner in his pine-panelled room. It boasted a small balcony which overlooked the lake and he stood out there for a while, staring across the blue-black water. It mirrored the darkness of its imprisoning mountains, stretching south to the distant hills of Montana; the craggy west face of Mount Crandell, part of the eastern escarpment of the Rockies, loomed black against the night sky yet Ben consciously saw little of it. Tomorrow morning he would be driving through the criss-cross streets fringed with pine and aspen, and he would be asking for Mrs Ellen Pearl.

And she would be talking about Joanna.

The northern end of Waterton Park village petered out towards a road that ran away from the valley and the lake to drag itself up across the lowering hills. It was not a good road, not a well-used road, for it had been by-passed by a bridge some three hundred yards below the scarp slope and a road which sliced through more photogenic scenery at the north-west bend of the lake. The traffic running along the lower road was busy; here, on the upper road Ben's was the only car, and perhaps this was symptomatic of the general situation and accounted for the air of seediness that hung over the service station where he pulled up.

There was a young lad at the pumps.

'Is this where the Pearls live?'

'Yup.' The overalled youngster gestured with his thumb in the direction of the house and returned to reading his paperback book. Ben drove the car forward towards the garage and parked beside it. The doors were open, there were three cars inside, one of them being worked on by another young man in greasy overalls. Ben hesitated, then walked over and tapped him on the shoulder.

'I'm looking for Mrs Ellen Pearl.'

The young man glanced up and wiped a greasy hand across his mouth.

'You better see Billy at the house.'

Ben nodded and left the garage for the house. It needed a coat of paint, and the wooden steps outside the door creaked loudly as they took his weight. His knocking was eventually answered by a stocky man of about forty, clad in overalls like the other men Ben had met, but with hands and face clean. It was a nice face, a round, gentle face that at the moment was shaded by a certain anxiety.

'Yeah? What can I do for you?'

'I'm looking for Mrs Ellen Pearl.'

'I'm Billy Pearl. What can I do for you?'

'It's your mother I really want to see.'

The brown eyes narrowed as they stared at Ben.

'Wait a minute. Are you the feller she wrote to, the one who sent a cable to say that he was comin' to see her?'

'That's right. My name's Ben South.'

The faint anxiety deepened to gloom, and Billy Pearl shook his head.

'I'm sorry about that. It kinda looks as though you're gonna have a wasted journey. Still, you better come in.'

The house was sparsely furnished but everything was clean and neat, and the pine panelling shone with a dull glow.

'Drink?'

'Not this early, thanks.'

Billy Pearl made no attempt to get a drink

himself, but motioned Ben to a chair and dropped into a deep rocking-chair near the fireplace. He watched Ben for a moment, and shook his head slowly.

'You come all the way from England? I'm real sorry about that.'

'How do you mean?'

'If you'd come only a couple days sooner, maybe, it would have been all right, but now... Point is, Mr South, the old lady got took bad on Saturday night, and she had a stroke. No, she's not dead, but she's down at the hospital right now and she's paralysed down her right side, can't move a muscle that side and her face is kinda twisted.' He broke off, and his brown eyes began to film over. 'Don't like to see her like that, she was always so active, you know, and for her to get like that, it must be causing her considerable mental pain.'

He looked up at Ben, collecting himself and his emotions.

'Yet that ain't so, either. Mental pain, I mean. The doctors, they tell me she ain't doin' much thinkin' right now. Fact is, she don't understand what's happened, or what's happening. She's in a coma, and they don't think she'll pull out of it – but even if she does, she ain't going to be good for much. They think that part of her brain's been destroyed, but I don't reckon to know too much about that kinda stuff. From your point of view, anyway, the fact is you've made a wasted journey because she just ain't going to be able to talk to you.' He hesitated, sheepishly. 'I did try to get through to you, to stop you comin' but what with it all blowin' up in the way it did, I was a bit late, and then once you were here in the country there didn't seem much point in going to all the chasing to contact you, and stoppin' you come to the Park anyway. It's a beautiful place, ain't it?'

Ben nodded. An immense disappointment washed over him, sharpened by the futility of his trip and the bad jolt his anticipated clearing up of the mystery of the letter's contents had taken. He frowned at his hands.

'Your mother wrote to me.'

'That's right. It's why you come to see her.'

'What did she have to tell me, do you know?'

Billy Pearl slung one foot over the other and began to rock the chair fretfully. He stared at his boots.

'That's a bit difficult to answer, Mr South. The straight answer is, I don't, and that'll be disappointing to you. But outside that there's the fact that maybe I *should* know, maybe I got a right to know, so I'd like to get the answers as much as you. I tell you, it's been hell for the old lady since Dad died. He told her somethin', kinda unburdened himself, I guess, and she's been through a tough time since. Maybe ... you think it had somethin' to do with her stroke, perhaps, all this worryin' she's done?'

'I don't know. What was she worrying about?'

'Something about Dad, something he did, I reckon, a few years back, afore we got here to the Park.'

'And you've no idea what it was?'

'Can't say I have.'

'You don't know how it was connected with ... with my wife?'

'No. I don't. The old lady didn't tell me a thing, but I knew she was shamed about something and hurt about whatever Dad did.'

'You say it must have happened before you got here. Where were you living before you came to the Park?'

'Well, we was in Alberta, just west of Red Deer in a place called–'

'Fairmont.'

'You know it? Well–'

Billy stopped, staring at Ben uncertainly. He had recognized the tenseness of his visitor's jaw and he was disturbed. He was a sensitive man, and one who took other people's troubles upon his own shoulders. His mouth drooped.

'That means somethin' to you, fact we came from Fairmont?'

'It's where my wife died, seven years ago.'

Billy Pearl was silent, staring again at his boots and shuffling his fingers over a stomach that was beginning to thicken to a generous paunch.

'The old lady was real worried.'

'Her letter suggested that ... whatever your father did had some connection with my wife.'

Billy cleared his throat noisily and rubbed an embarrassed hand against his jaw.

'Look, Mr South, like I say I don't know a thing about all this, and the old lady kept it to herself, just the same way Dad kept it to hisself these years gone. But I think you gotta realize it may not be serious enough to warrant you spendin' too much time on it.'

'Serious?'

'By your lights, I mean,' Billy added hastily. 'I ain't implyin' that the old lady would bring you right across here for nuthin', it's just that her ... her standards wouldn't necessarily be the same as yours. Heck, I'm not makin' this out well. Fact is,' he went on in some desperation, 'she was an old lady and she was brought up in a hard school where there just wasn't any messin' about with moral standards, you know what I mean? You could tell a man's worth by the times he went to church, you see, and she was a strict one, out of the old stock down in Utah and Dad became a Mormon when he married her in the States but he was never as keen on it as she was. Yet they say converts are always the strictest, don't they? That wasn't so with them; the old lady stayed a stickler to the end. Me, I was softer, like Dad, I guess.'

He looked sheepish at the admission and was silent. Ben leaned forward slowly in his chair.

'You're trying to say that your father's action might not have been as blameworthy, as serious as your mother made out.'

'It was sure on her conscience, it was that serious. But she was getting near the grave you know, and religion and principle gets tough to face when that's so.'

'I know what you mean.' Ben hesitated. 'How long did you live in Fairmont?'

'Fair number of years. I was born there. Dad had a job in town as the head of the service department at one of the car dealers, and got along pretty well. Better than we did out here at the Park.'

'How did you come to move here?'

'Well, about five, six years ago Dad made a hit on the horses – gosh, the old lady raised hell about it, said he'd go to the devil playin' the horses, but she agreed to use it in a good cause when we upped and moved outa Fairmont and came across here to open this garage.'

He scratched himself reflectively.

'Allus surprised me that Dad wanted to

leave Red Deer and Fairmont; he'd spent a long time there. He must have had more'n his share of ants bitin' him just then. I mean, playin' the horses suddenly and then chuckin' everythin' to come here to the Park, and open his own place. I suppose he had the money, and it was better, havin' his own place I mean.'

'I gathered from Mrs Pearl's letter that things hadn't gone well recently.'

'You can say that again. No sooner we moved here and got started than they began buildin' that lower road down below and it pulled all the traffic from this track up here. Trade dropped back, and now it's just mostly local stuff we get.' He wiggled his boots sadly. 'The old lady's been sayin', these last few weeks, it's just a judgment of Heaven on the old man.'

'How long has he been dead?'

'Three months now.'

It had taken Mrs Pearl that long to decide to write to Ben South. It must have been a struggle: her own moral standards and shame at her husband's conduct battling with the fearful decision to tell a stranger of the infamy of the man she'd loved for more than forty years. Infamy. A strange word for Ben to apply to the conduct of the dead man. Perhaps it would have been infamy to Mrs Pearl, but that wasn't to say Ben would think it so.

'I'm sorry I can't help you more, Mr

South,' Billy Pearl said, breaking the uncomfortable silence. 'But the old lady jus' kept it to herself.'

Ben glanced around, and stood up.

'I'm grateful for your time, Mr Pearl. But–' he hesitated, reluctant to give the matter up entirely – 'is there nothing? I mean is there the chance your father might have kept some record of his action? Whatever it was?'

'Could be, Mr South, but can't say for sure.' Billy rose to his feet and began to walk towards the back of the house. 'Come along with me, and see what I mean.'

He opened the screen door at the back and gestured across a derelict yard to the wood shed with the galvanized iron roof. He led the way to the door and then moved to the window, rubbing at its grimy surface.

'The old lady's got the key somewhere, but this is what I mean. She made him put all this stuff out here, best part of a year ago. Clutter.'

Ben peered through the window and saw the piles of cardboard boxes on the floor and table. There seemed to be hundreds of them, piled high, stained and yellow and grimy.

'What are they?'

'Huh! The old man was a hoarder. He worked on the principle you never know when a thing'll come in useful, and you never know when someone's gonna challenge you on a transaction you undertook years back.

He saved everythin' – and I mean everythin'. Paper, souvenirs, medals he won as a kid, invoices, bills of sale, turkey shoot tickets, boy, you name it, he kept it. Now I tell you, there may be somethin', and if it exists, it's in there. But don't ask me to look for it!'

And it might not even be important. Ben walked back across the yard behind Billy. England was a long way away, and Joanna's image had arisen in his mind to torture him, and for this. Nothing. An old lady's out-raged moral or religious principle?

'Do you mind if I call in to see her?'

'No, sir. She won't hear you or anythin'. But you can call. She's at the Cardston Hos-pital. I'll ring them, tell them you're coming.'

Ben thanked him and shook hands. As he drove away he saw Billy Pearl standing near the pumps. The chubby man gave a sad, embarrassed wave of his hand and in his driving mirror Ben could see him watching the car, disconsolately.

At last the shoulder of the hill hid Billy Pearl and the garage from view.

There was no trouble at the Cardston Hospital. Ben was allowed to go to the room occupied by Mrs Pearl. A nurse stood beside him as he stared at the weak, stiff figure in the bed. Ellen Pearl was about sixty-five years old, he calculated, and the stroke she'd suffered had drawn in her cheeks and hol-lowed her eyes. The only movement he could see was the pulse that beat in her temple. Her eyes were open but she saw nothing.

He knew now she would never tell him why she had found it necessary to write half-way across the world, to a stranger, to say that in her eyes her husband had committed a sin.

Ben walked out into the sunshine and went back to his car. He thought of England, and the office, and he saw the saw-toothed, sunlit white border of the mountains of Montana, a towering wall of rock, and he turned the key for the car engine to roar to life. He'd come back to Canada, but he'd reached a dead-end, and Joanna's ghost still hovered in his mind. Perhaps it was time to exorcize her, time to do the things he should have done seven years ago. He hadn't had the courage then, but time had given him courage and the incentive.

Fairmont, and Red Deer lay north.

2

He had four days left to him before he took his plane back to England. When he reached Calgary he took a room and over dinner worked out what his next steps should be. First, he decided he would get in touch with the police at Fairmont and try to obtain some information about his wife's death from

41

them: seven years later than he should have done. And then there was Mary Davis. It would mean a trip up to Red Deer to see her, but he had never got in touch with her since Joanna died. It was not so much that he thought she would now be able to give him information about Joanna; it was just that he wanted to talk to her about his dead wife, bring some semblance of order to the whirling emotions that troubled his senses – and make up in some way for the long silence from him. It could only have upset her. They had never met, but she would have expected him to get in touch with her after Joanna died. His father had talked to her but that wasn't enough. Ben South could now make up for an omission of seven years' standing.

He obtained both numbers from directory enquiries and rang the police first. After he explained what he wanted to three different people he was finally put in touch with a Captain McGregor. The captain was doubtful.

'I'm not sure we c'n help you, Mr South. You say you were the dead woman's husband?'

'That's right. Really, it would be a help if I could just talk, in the first instance, with the officers who handled the case.'

'S'a long time, y'know. Still, we got the records. Ya say you'll be through this way?'

'That's right. I'm speaking from Calgary;

with an early start tomorrow I could get to see you in the afternoon.'

'Okay, you stop by here tomorrow afternoon and I'll see you and we'll have a get-together on this. Right?'

A few minutes later Ben got through to Mary Davis's home in Red Deer. A man answered the phone.

'Hello? Is that Mr Davis? My name's South – Ben South.'

'Yeah?'

'I … your wife, Mary – she was friendly at one time with my wife. Joanna South.'

There was a silence broken only by the heavy breathing of the man at the other end of the line. Ben waited and was about to speak again when the man finally replied.

'I'm Seth Davis. Mary's in the kitchen. Maybe you ought to speak to her.'

The phone rattled and there was a scuffling sound. Ben wondered briefly at the brusqueness in Seth Davis's voice when he had spoken, and then considered that perhaps it was occasioned by the fact that Ben South's name would not be a very popular one with the Davis family. Mary would have been hurt by his refusal to communicate, all these years…

'Hello?'

The voice had a tremulous, uncertain quality.

'Mary … Mary Davis? This is Ben South.

We ... we spoke on the telephone a couple of times, some years ago.'

Lame, inadequate; but for some reason Ben's heart was beating quickly.

'Jo's husband. Yes, Ben, I remember. It's such a long time since... How are you?'

'I'm well. I've been living in England since ... since Joanna died. I'm over here now, for a week, and I'm driving up from Calgary tomorrow and I thought–'

'Can you come and see us?'

Her tones had become livelier, as though she felt herself on safer ground suddenly. 'It would be great if you could, Ben. We'd love to see you – we never met, and Jo, she used to talk about you so much. She... I'm sorry, Ben, I never did get to telling you how shattered we all were when–'

'That's all right, Mary; it was my fault, for running away from it all. But now I'd like to come, to meet you, and talk with you. I really would.'

'That's marvellous. We're going to be up at Valley Fork tomorrow seeing some friends but why not come see us on Thursday? Can you stay with us, overnight?'

Ben protested that such hospitality wasn't necessary but Mary Davis insisted and seemed delighted with his acceptance. Just before the call ended Seth Davis came back on the phone and apologized briefly for being so brusque earlier.

'I just wasn't with it, Ben; I hadn't realized who you were. Anyways, we look forward to seeing you. Thursday.'

So it was fixed. And yet Ben was still left with the impression that Seth Davis's brusqueness had not been occasioned by a failure to realize who Ben South was. He shrugged the thought aside, and undressed for an early shower. An early shower, an early bed, an early start in the morning.

Next morning Ben edged his car out along Eighth Avenue and past the stampede grounds. Within the hour he was clear of the city and picking up speed in contrast to the rush-hour traffic crawling into Calgary bumper to bumper.

But he was heading north.

To the west the powerful line of the Rockies ran north with him, their white-tipped peaks gleaming in the morning sunshine, blue-etched against a bluer sky. He paid little attention to the view; he was driving north and the years were rolling back from him as he drove, for he had lived and worked in Alberta and he had brought his wife to Edmonton, and somewhere up there, in the distant blue hills ahead of him, she had died.

He reached Fairmont at noon. It was a typical small boom town, spawning from the work provided by the sulphur creek that he passed on the way down from the hills. He'd stopped briefly at the creek to stare at the

45

golden wall of brimstone that damned a scarlet lake of liquid sulphur in the huge storage block, and he'd seen the men scrambling over the yellow block, drilling holes to crack a shipment for the processing plant. He'd driven on down to the town and recognized the scattering of houses and straight streets. He'd never been to Fairmont before but he'd seen Fairmont wherever oil, or gas, or uranium had been discovered.

He visited the police department after lunch.

Captain McGregor was a tall, rawboned man with a shining head that was entirely devoid of hair. His uniform was strained tightly across the shoulders and chest as he leaned back in his chair and stared at Ben with thinly disguised curiosity. He clucked his tongue and gave a shake of his head in surprise.

'You tellin' me you came all the way from England, jus' to talk to us about somethin' that happened seven years ago?'

'I didn't talk to you about it then.'

'Took you a long time to get roun' to it, Mr South. And it seems to me that we aren't goin' to be able to help you too much either.'

'You said you had records.'

'Well, thass so, but seven years is a long time. We got the records all right and we can show you the story and the details that are on file, but you said you was hopin' to be able to talk to some of the officers, and that jus' isn't possible.'

'Why not?'

'Mr South, you must remember this isn't a big city department. Our strength isn't high, and a few years back you'd have seen the old timers jus' payin' out their time on the job. The fact is, when your wife died out here three officers went out to the valley. I wasn't around, those days, by the way; I only came in when Selly Gargan got crushed by that rock. He was one of the officers you'd be wantin' to see. He was up doin' some fishin' at Jasper Park they tell me, and he got caught in a rock fall. Five years off retirin' too.'

'And Gargan investigated my wife's death?'

'Ahuh. He wasn't in charge, though. Investigating officer was an experienced feller, name of Sam Durrance. Now he moved down to Shelby, Montana, some five years back. They tell me he's got folks down there.'

'Retired?'

'No, I guess not. The fellers here don't seem to know what he's doin' now. He didn't keep in touch, jus' upped and went they tell me, said he was fed to the teeth with the job and went south. He wasn't near retirin' – he'd be around fifty now, they say. The third officer, he was retired. Got a place up on High River. I knew him. Tom Corey. He won't help you much though; he got caught up in a fracas down at the sulphur

47

creek two years back when some of them miners got to whoopin' it up and he came a crack across the skull. He was glad to retire soon after; never could remember much about anythin' after that crack. I rang him this morning about your wife, but he don't recall it, or anythin' about it. You can blame those sulphur miners for that, those boys...'

He scratched his left ear sadly and shook his head. Ben stared out of the window.

'I passed the sulphur creek as I came in,' he said dully.

'You can't miss it. Used to be the only thing booming this town but there's the Fenokee Project now too.'

'Fenokee Project?'

'The complex of dams up in the hills. There's a pile of money gone into that feller, believe me; wish I had a slice of it. Some of them boys come down here on a Saturday night, though most of them go on up to Red Deer. You should see that Project. Man, it's somethin'!'

Ben was hardly listening. He was thinking that the doors were continually closing. First Mrs Pearl, then these three officers, all unavailable or unable to help him in his search. Search for what? He didn't know, suddenly. Mrs Pearl had written in guarded tones and here he was in Canada on what was turning out to be an aimless quest.

'Anyways, I'd better let you see the files,

since you come all that way. Can't turn you away with nothing.'

Captain McGregor spoke quietly on the phone, replaced the receiver and watched Ben with curious grey eyes. Ben said nothing.

A few minutes later a brown file was in Ben's hands. McGregor sat quietly in his chair, one lean hand placed on the desk, the grey eyes watching Ben as he read the papers in the file. They consisted of reports submitted by the officers. They were sparse in detail. There was also a brief note of the inquest. As Ben lifted the sheet to read it McGregor said quietly,

'You been up there yet?'

'Where?'

'Fairmont Valley.'

'No.'

'Pretty drive. And an expensive one. Millionaire belt. But your wife wouldn't've been driving there for the scenery. Seems like she took the wrong road at Valley Fork and ended up wrong side of the hill for Fairmont. So they said at the inquest.' He hesitated, watching Ben closely. 'Understandable, that mistake, if she hadn't been to Red Deer or Fairmont before.'

'She had.'

'You say? Hmm. Still, the weather was bad, wasn't it? She could've missed the turning in the snow. Tough. If she'd made the right turning away from Fairmont, she'd have got to Red Deer all right and you wouldn't be here now. But that's the way of the world, Mr South.'

Ben avoided looking at the captain, though he detected the sympathy in the man's voice, ill-phrased though it might have been. He read the inquest report.

'The transcript here is short.'

'It is. All that was necessary for the file. Don't tell me you'd like to see the full one! It's the courthouse records'll hold that.'

'Yes. I won't bother with it.' Ben stood up and handed the file back to the police captain. 'Doesn't seem to be much more I can get here. The whole thing's been, well, a waste of time, I guess. I'm sorry to have troubled you.'

McGregor shrugged. A frown masked his brow.

'Your time, Mr South.'

Ben hesitated as he began to turn towards the door. Something had begun to nag at him and he couldn't place it, couldn't define it in his mind. He stared at McGregor and the captain raised his eyebrows.

'Something bothering you?'

'The officers ... they'd have given evidence at the inquest? They'd have given the evidence in the transcript?'

'Not all of them. Sam Durrance, as investigatin' officer, he'd have given evidence.'

'There'd have been other witnesses.'

'Sure. Expert witnesses would've been called in. But as I recall from the file there were only two called.'

'I saw no names mentioned on the file.'

'You're wrong, surely!'

McGregor thumbed through the file then scratched his ear thoughtfully. He stood up, carrying the file and walked towards the door.

'It was here this mornin'... I'd better check in the file-room myself.'

Ben heard McGregor speaking in the outer office. He waited, and there was a strange prickling at the back of his neck. He was on edge, his nerves were suddenly strained and he wasn't quite sure why. He quivered as McGregor suddenly appeared in the doorway. The officer was holding a sheet of paper in his hand and there was a satisfied expression on his lean face.

'I knew I was right; I'd seen the list this morning. It was there all right but when the clerk put the file back the punch hole got torn and this lodged in the filing cabinet. Here y'are, witnesses. Like I said, apart from Sam Durrance there were jus' two of them.'

Ben took the sheet of paper from him and stared at it. The composition of the inquest and the venue were stated along with the date and time. Below was the name of Police Sergeant S. Durrance, called to give evidence concerning the site of the accident and the discovery of the body. Her body. Then came an unfamiliar name. Dr G Nebbia, called to state the cause of death. But Ben's eyes slipped past to the third of the names on the sheet and he knew why his neck had begun to prickle in anticipation.

The third witness had been an expert called to give evidence relating to the car. He was named as Mr J Pearl.

3

Graham Nebbia gazed with satisfaction out of his office window. The morning sun was gleaming on the bright green lawns that ran down in a gentle slope from the main building of the nursing home and sparkling on the miniature pool that had been stocked with fish only this summer. There were two patients down there already, old Mrs Boyer and that fool Maxim, always wanting to talk about the old days when he'd pioneered in Nebraska before coming north to make his fortune in oil. Nebbia snorted in contempt and turned away, putting on his white coat and stepping across to the full-length mirror that hung behind the cloak cupboard in the corner of his large office.

He adjusted the coat across his shoulders and contemplated the image in the mirror. At fifty-two Graham Nebbia still possessed a youthful figure and his face had the leanness that could be fascinating to young women. Not that many of his patients were young, it was only the older ones who could afford his fees, the older ones, the widowed ones, the dying ones who sought an elixir and paid for a chimera with good, hard cash. And paid gratefully as Graham Nebbia leaned across them, and warmed them with his eyes, and touched their hands with his dry, hard fingers.

He stepped closer to the mirror and adjusted his plain silk tie, then inspected his skin closely and critically. His pores had not yet become enlarged, and there was no trace of extra flesh along his jawline. Life had been good to Graham Nebbia, and was still being so – his appearance, the Parkland Nursing Home, the way the waiting list for his services grew – yes, life was good. He smiled at the mirror and the sound white teeth grinned in reflection.

He turned at the knock on his door and closed the cloak cupboard.

'Yes?'

Mrs Anderson entered. As usual her starched uniform was immaculate and he nodded, pleased. She was carrying his appointments book under her arm.

'Your appointments for the morning, Dr Nebbia. May I remind you that you will need to leave by twelve-thirty at the latest, to get to the convention this evening? Your plane leaves at three.'

'Thank you, Mrs Anderson. I'll be all through by twelve, I'm sure. Now the first lady who wishes to–'

Mrs Anderson interrupted him and he was surprised. In the even tenor of their business relationship Mrs Anderson never interrupted him.

'There is a young man who wishes to see you, Dr Nebbia.'

'Without an appointment?'

'Yes, Doctor. He's very insistent.' A red spot had appeared on Mrs Anderson's cheek; she was aware of Dr Nebbia's cold surprise. 'He says that it is very important that he gets to see you this morning.'

'This morning?'

'Immediately.'

'What's his reason?'

'He says that it's private and confidential, Doctor.'

'All right then, his name.'

'South, Mr Ben South.'

Graham Nebbia shook his head impatiently, and turned away to his desk.

'I know of no one of that name. Why couldn't he make an appointment in the normal manner? Tell him to arrange another convenient time and–'

'He says he's come all the way from England, Dr Nebbia.'

54

Graham Nebbia stared at her in surprise. This young man must have impressed Mrs Anderson with a sense of urgency for her to interrupt her employer twice in one morning. He sighed and sat down behind his desk.

'All right. You'd better show him in. I'll give him ten minutes and no more because I have a schedule to keep to as you well know. Go on, Mrs Anderson, show this Mr … er…'

'South.'

'…South in, and…'

Graham Nebbia's voice died away and he sat stiffly behind his desk, staring at Mrs Anderson as though he had never seen her in his life before and hadn't been expecting to. His lips moved after a few moments, framing the word, the name she had given him, but no sound came. Mrs Anderson waited and then began to walk towards the door.

'Shall I show him in, Doctor?'

A strangled sound preceded the one sharp word he spoke.

'*No!*'

Mrs Anderson looked back at him in surprise. Graham Nebbia's face was pale and he was leaning forward across his desk urgently, with both fists clenched. She took a step towards him. 'Are you all right, Dr Nebbia?'

He sat back as though she had slapped him and colour at once flooded back into his face, yet he still looked sick.

'All right? Of course I am! This man … this Mr South, tell him I'm not available this morning!'

'But you said–'

'I'm not available!'

The words were snapped out viciously and Graham Nebbia's mouth was set in a tight angry line as he glared at her wildly. Her head came up.

'All right, Doctor, as you wish. I'll tell him to make an appointment.'

She walked out and closed the door behind her with an exaggerated care. Graham Nebbia remained where he was for a little while, staring fixedly at his hands, then slowly he rose and walked across to the window. This time he did not stand fully in the embrasure but remained to one side, stationed beside the curtain with his cheek close to the glass. From this vantage point he could see the small car park beyond the lawns.

He stood there without moving for at least ten minutes before he saw the stranger entering the park. He saw a man in a dark suit, a well set-up, broad-shouldered man, with hair that looked black in the sunlight. He was walking purposefully towards a car in the park. When he reached it he stood beside it for a long moment, staring back towards the nursing home, and there was anger in every line of his body. At last he got in the car, and drove away.

Graham Nebbia went back to his desk and sat down. Mrs Anderson knocked and came in. She was looking upset, and her colour was heightened.

'He was a very insistent young man. He caused a scene in reception. We actually had to bar the way! Really, Doctor Nebbia, I–'

'No appointments this morning,' Nebbia said huskily. 'Cancel them.'

'I beg your pardon, Doctor? There are three–'

'*Cancel them!* What's the matter with you today, Mrs Anderson? Do I have to say every-thing twice? *Cancel the damned appointments!*'

He hardly saw her go, trailing indignation like a comet tail of affronted efficiency. He sat behind the desk for almost an hour un-able to think clearly. Then he rose and began to prowl around the room. He glanced at his watch. To hell with the convention! He had a headache. He'd go home, lie down.

Ben South.

He stopped. He stared at the wall. He walked to his desk and picked up the tele-phone. The girl on his switchboard cut in immediately.

'I want you to get me a number,' he said. 'It's Mr James P–' He stopped, and stared at the receiver as though it were red hot. 'Never mind.'

He replaced the receiver and paced the room. He whipped off his white coat and threw it on the chair. He walked out of the office without his hat and went straight to his car, leaving no instructions with Mrs Anderson. He drove quickly down the hill until he came to a drugstore on the outskirts of town. There was a pay phone there.

When he obtained the number from the operator he dialled it, bracing his back against the door of the booth. Seven years, God, it was seven years!

There was a voice at the other end of the line.

'Hello?' Graham Nebbia said. 'My name ... my name is Nebbia. I want to speak to Mr Haggett. That's right.' He ran his tongue over lips that were suddenly dry. 'Mr James P. Haggett.'

CHAPTER 3

1

A few miles outside Fairmont the road swung left and began to climb through low hills, dipped and swung in a long, slow curve before entering the pines of Fairmont Valley. Topping a rise, Ben could look up and across the valley to see a winding river, blue under the summer sky, drifting below a grey bluff wreathed at its shoulders with pine and aspen. Sand banks lurched up on the east bank of the river and above them he caught a glimpse of occasional houses, red-timbered, nestling among the trees and protected by the slopes. Then the view was gone as the car nosed its way into the shadow of the thick trees and the road took him back nearer the valley floor, but winding still up towards the distant, snow-capped peaks that heralded the Columbia Icefield, the hundred square mile remnant of the last Ice Age, straddling and embracing the Continental Divide. In the far distance he could see Mount Athabasca and he recalled the one occasion when he had gone there, to thread the crevasses in a sight-seeing snowmobile – skis replacing front wheels, endless treads providing traction. He could remember the bright orange of the snowmobiles, the whiteness of the snow, the blue of the sky.

It had been the summer before he met Joanna.

And she had died here, in this valley, this quiet, peaceful valley where the road wound gracefully along under shadowing trees, where a late summer sun burned high in a blue sky, where one could drive through a coulée scented with wild rose and come across a ranch cabin thrust under a towering wall of rock, rising so abruptly from the trees that the green branches seemed to break against it in waves and its raw, crude beauty assaulted the senses. Joanna had died here, somewhere along this road, unseen, unnoticed by passing motorists, on her knees in the snow, under the trees.

In a parking area on the top of a hill he stopped the car and got out. The valley lay below him with its expensive week-end houses and its bright river. He crossed the road, turning his back on the river and climbed the slope, pushing his way through low bush as dense as the hair on a dog's back. As he climbed, scratching his hands, grabbing for purchase, the bush opened to give way to shale and outcroppings of limestone. He was under the lee of a high peak and on its slope he could see a knee-high forest, aspen and cottonwood that would be perhaps two hundred years old, dwarfed by the cold dry wind that would funnel down through the pass above the valley. In winter that wind would become boisterous, strong enough to lift a man bodily or force him down to his stomach to escape the shrapnel-like shale that would be jetted along in its wake. But Joanna wouldn't have known that wind for she had died in the silence below, the cold white silence of the river bank. McGregor had said the car was fifty feet from the river and she must have staggered along among the trees unable to climb the slope in her dazed state.

She wouldn't have seen this valley in the summer. She wouldn't have seen the low meadows blazing with colour, two-inch-high cushion pinks, purple gentian, yellow cinquefoil, flowers thick in the shadows. And now she'd never see the way pollen blew from the lodgepines so that it looked like smoke, and she wouldn't see the pine thinning to fir, and the fir to grass, and the grass to moss, until there was only the hard, proud rock, encrusted lime-green and orange with lichen.

She would have seen just the snow. And at the inquest there had been just Joe Pearl, and Dr Nebbia, and Sam Durrance to speak her epitaph.

But they weren't speaking now. Joe Pearl dead and his secret locked in the iron-clamped lips of his stricken widow, Sam Durrance across the border in Shelby, Montana, and Nebbia ... from Nebbia a straight, contemptuous refusal. Ben sat down on the shale and stared into the valley. He was inclined to give up for there was a lassitude creeping over him. Each way he turned, each step he took, he was reminded again of his dead wife, but each reminder was so pointless, so useless, for he was learning nothing. There was only the souring of suspicion creeping into his mind until even this valley looked evil in the sunlight.

Evil, and yet there was only an unnamed

suspicion in his mind, a suspicion that his wife's death had left questions unanswered, questions that he should have pressed seven years ago. Questions that he could not press then because of his emotional collapse, and that he found difficulty in pressing now because of the lapse of time.

And because men like McGregor could get angry at insinuations, at suggestions of corruption.

The sun was burning the side of his face before he went back to the car. He drove on through the valley, until he reached Valley Fork. The sign pointed to Red Deer.

2

The house had a gravel turn-off and was set back over the ridge of a low hill. The building itself was timber, long and sprawling in construction, and the wide board steps outside led to a veranda where he could see a weather-beaten hickory rocking-chair, and some comfortable looking garden furniture. He parked the car and walked slowly towards the house. As he reached the steps the screen door opened and a woman stood framed in the doorway, staring at him. She was short, and rather plump, dressed in a grey skirt and bright red sweater that was drawn tight at the waist, accentuating her figure. Her hair was black, curling short to frame her heart-shaped face and her bright, lively eyes were wide spaced and eager.

'Ben?' she said in the uncertain voice he had heard over the telephone and he walked up the steps holding out his hand.

'You're Mary.'

For a moment she hesitated, almost took his hand but then impulsively rushed forward to throw her arms around him and reach up to kiss his cheek. When she stepped back her face was flushed and he was grinning.

'It's a long time since I had a welcome like that!'

'I feel like we're old friends, Ben, so it gives me the right to kiss you welcome. When Jo stayed here with us she spent most of the time talking about you so it's like I know you, and have known you for years. But come in, don't let's stand here, come in and meet Seth.'

He was standing just inside the door, nodding his head, smiling, extending a horny hand to grasp Ben's. He was about Ben's age and barrel-chested. He had bright red hair that lay in tight curls low on his forehead and the deep cleft in his chin gave his broad face a reliable, powerful look. He was far from handsome, and his skin was leathery from exposure to the sun and wind but his eyes were a smoky brown, soft and friendly. His handgrip was firm and positive.

'It's great to meet you at last, Ben.'

'And you, Seth.'

'You have a good trip from Calgary?'

'Well, I made it along to Fairmont in reasonable time.'

'You stopped off in Fairmont, then?' Seth asked, leading the way through to the long sitting-room with its panelled walls and open hearth. He gestured Ben to an easy-chair and leaned against the chimney while Mary came in behind them.

'I stopped off overnight, saw a few people. Or didn't see them, as the case may be.'

'Huh?'

Mary bustled forward, interrupting them.

'You had lunch, Ben? Good. Well, we'll be eating in a couple of hours but if you're hungry after your drive I can fix you something. Or do you settle for tea, English style? You know, I've never been to England, you must tell me all about it. I mean, is it true that–'

'Heck,' Seth said with a grin. 'I'll get your traps in while you satisfy my wife's yearning for travel.'

He walked out to the car and strangely enough Mary stopped her chatter at once to eye Ben seriously.

'Before Seth comes back, let me say this, Ben. I was very fond of Joanna, I loved her. We were both shattered when she died, for Seth liked her a lot too, but we've never talked much about it, because we were both upset at the time. I think he's worried now about what you've got to say to us so I'm getting in now, before he comes back. If there was anything we could have done–'

'Mary, please, I know the way you felt about her. And I know there was no question of blame on your part at all. I guess you'll have been worried about my long silence, never coming to see you. I wasn't blaming you, and Seth; I just broke up that's all, and I couldn't think, couldn't act. In the end I just ran.'

She leaned across and squeezed his hand.

'I know. Your father told me, when he called to see us, after the inquest.'

Seth clumped in with the bags and stood in the doorway looking at them.

'Hey, hey! Holding hands already?'

It was good to be with them. He realized now just how great a mistake it had been not to come to them when Joanna had died. Here he could have found sympathy and understanding, for Mary possessed it in abundance and she had loved his wife. Over dinner she told him many stories of the way they had grown up together and all three laughed at the recounting. She told Ben of the blind dates they had gone on back in Ontario, and the holidays they had spent together. After dinner Seth lit his pipe and the three of them sat out on the veranda in the cool evening watching the stars come up. The Davises lived on the edge of town, in what Ben reckoned was an expensive area – and still the talk was mainly from Mary, about Joanna. For Ben it brought no pain, but an addition to the warm memories that he held of his dead wife. The pain was eased, almost erased as he listened. Mary sighed.

'Of course, when Dad left Ontario I didn't see much of Jo for a while. I met this big lug here, working at a building site near the sawmill he was, and Dad nearly blew a vein when he heard I was going out with him. Then Jo wrote to tell me she was marrying some gorgeous hunk called Ben South. I was mad. So I up and married this feller here, and lived to regret it ever since.'

Her tone belied the words, as did her glance, affectionately bestowed upon her husband. He sat nodding, drawing on his pipe, and smiling in the dimness.

'Then a couple of years later,' Mary continued, 'I had a letter from her to say that she was moving to Edmonton, and could she call to see us from time to time. Seth here will tell you how excited I got.'

'Ever have apple pie and ice-cream spilled down the back of your neck? That's how excited she got!'

'You didn't need it anyway, you were getting too fat. As you are now, Seth Davis. Anyway, Jo came down to see us several times and it was great having her. And then...'

The night was silent and a light breeze sprang up, touching Ben's cheek with cool fingers. He stared up at the stars, spattered like jewels in a woman's dark hair. A car engine coughed into life, throbbing in the silence.

'And now you're back,' Mary said softly. 'It's been a long time. I ... I often wondered whether you'd married again.'

Ben shook his head. There had been that period of time when he'd dated Carol Taylor, when he thought that maybe it would be possible. But that was in the past, Joanna's shadow still loomed large in his life, and there was nothing he could say to Seth and Mary that would make sense to them. But maybe they were sensitive enough to realize he could say nothing. Even so, Mary didn't allow the matter to lie.

'I don't believe Jo would have wanted you to just hang on to memories, Ben.'

'Maybe not.'

'I think she was the kind of girl who'd appreciate that a man can't carry a torch for ever. What do you say, Seth?'

'Huh? Heck, I don' know.' He grinned suddenly and shifted in his chair. 'Seems like you women are never satisfied till you get a feller married off.'

Mary didn't return the smile. In a level

67

tone she said,

'When two people have a good thing going, as Ben and Jo did, I think it's just natural that they should want to try to repeat it, if one dies.'

They sat in silence for a while until Seth suggested that Ben might like a drink. He retuned a few minutes later with a bottle of whisky and he and Ben sat drinking while Mary hugged her knees thoughtfully on the veranda step, her face in profile to Ben's. When Ben had almost finished his drink he suddenly said,

'You mentioned my father earlier, and the inquest. Did you go along?'

'I did,' Seth said after a pause. 'Mary was too upset, but I thought I ought to go along.'

'We felt badly about it, both of us. She was coming down to see us, but why she didn't phone I can't understand. I mean, the first thing we realized when we heard that she'd been found dead was that she must have been coming down to see us and then–'

'Perhaps she couldn't get through to you.'

'No, for some reason she just couldn't have phoned. Seth was home all that day, working on some survey statistics, and I was home all afternoon, after I'd been down town in the morning. She must have just packed up and driven down.'

'There's the possibility,' Ben said slowly,

'that she was upset. When I told her I couldn't get home that weekend she sounded rather … distant.'

'It was a long time ago, Ben. Don't torture yourself about it now. It's all over, and in the past.'

'Perhaps you're right.'

'Another drink, feller?' Seth poured a liberal dose of whisky into Ben's glass and settled back on the rocking-chair with a grunt. The chair needed oiling; it began to squeak as he rocked.

'You say you stopped off in Fairmont. Know folks there?'

Ben sipped at his glass thoughtfully. He was a little reluctant to involve the Davises in this but on the other hand they had been Joanna's friends, and they were his, and there was the possibility that they would be able to help him.

'Not exactly. Seth, you say you went to the inquest. Do you remember much about it?'

'Some.'

'Remember one of the witnesses? A man named Pearl?'

'Can't say I recall his name.'

'His widow wrote me a letter.' Ben recounted the story, omitting the part his own emotions had played in the matter in deciding to come to Canada, and went on to tell of his disappointments when the trails seemed to end blankly.

69

'I don't quite follow your drift,' Seth said doubtfully, fingering the deep cleft in his chin.

'I can't say the whole thing is any too clear to me. You see, Joe Pearl ran the service department of a car dealer in Fairmont. Now he picked up some fees on the side by acting as a police department expert on car maintenance and so on. It wasn't a regular arrangement, and maybe they should have used proper forensic people but it was a small force and this was a routine matter and Joe Pearl was respected locally. So he looked Jo's car over, and was called as a witness at the inquest.'

'Still can't say I remember him!'

'Probably because he said very little. He gave the car a clean bill of health and stated his opinion that she just skidded off the road. All right, now where does that leave us? The letter his widow wrote me implied he'd done something wrong and it was in some way connected with my wife. The only connection he did have with Joanna, that I know of, was in relation to the inquest – and giving evidence there. If Ellen Pearl talks of shame, could she have been saying that maybe her husband perjured himself at that inquest.'

'Hey, hold on, Ben!' Mary stared at him as Seth expostulated and rocked more quickly in his chair. 'That seems to be jumping a few fences!'

70

'So Captain McGregor thought. He almost got violent about it. With reason, perhaps. I guess I was maligning the Fairmont police department, and he had a right to get puce in the face. But it still seems logical to me. And then there's Nebbia, and Durrance.'

'The fact that you haven't spoken to Durrance is hardly his fault,' Mary said quietly. 'You've not approached him.'

'And this Nebbia feller – if he's a professional man he maybe just didn't have time to see you.'

They were right, of course, and he was on the defensive, but he still felt that something was wrong. He shook his head and took a stiff drink.

'Maybe I've just been affected by the mystery of Mrs Pearl's letter.'

'There's the chance she was cranky, you know, feller. You did say she was strong on her religion.'

'Yes. But it still bugs me, Seth. What other connection is there between Pearl and Joanna? How else could he have behaved "shamefully"?'

The rocking-chair had stopped squeaking and Seth was staring into the darkness.

'It's cold,' Mary said. 'Let's go indoors.'

Ben felt he had put a damper on the evening, for his host and hostess were strangely subdued. He himself found it difficult to start up a conversation again and it was with some relief that he heard Seth suggest they might catch the television newscast. Mary went through to the kitchen to make some fresh coffee.

The announcer was talking about an American senator named Roberts who was appearing before a congressional enquiry in relation to charges of corruption.

'They'll never make that stick,' Seth said dogmatically. 'That Roberts, he's a big wheel, and corruption is always what they try to pull on you down there if you're being too successful.'

'I can't say I've heard much about him.'

'Roberts? Say, where you been – all right, I know, England! Why, Roberts was one of the pushers in the Fenokee Project!'

'Captain McGregor mentioned that to me. What is it?'

Seth sat up, grinned, scratched his red thatch, leaned over to switch off the television control beside his chair then swivelled to stare at Ben.

'Say, you need educating. Look around you, boy, at this house! What's paying for it? The Fenokee Project!– Well, not directly, of course, because my connection isn't with the Project itself, but if it wasn't for Fenokee I wouldn't be working where I am. Hey, you're a surveyor–'

'*Was* a surveyor. Businessman, now.'

'Once was, always is,' Seth countered with

a swift grin. 'Come over here and I'll show you what you've been missing this last seven years.'

He walked across the room and opened a door that led to a small study. He switched on the light, yelled to Mary that she could bring the coffee through, and opened the filing cabinet against the wall. He brought out a roll of maps. The one he selected and spread out on the table, pushing aside other papers to do so, was a large-scale map of west Alberta.

'Now let me start from the beginning. This here is the Athabasca Glacier, and down here runs the tongue of the Columbia Icefield. About ten years ago the Research Council carried out a study of the mechanics of flow of the glacier. This tongue of ice marked here melts into the Arctic Ocean by way of the Athabasca River; these other tongues send their waters down to the Pacific through the Columbia, and to Hudson Bay by way of the Saskatchewan River.'

'Ahuh. I can see that.'

'Fine. So what, you ask? So this. The Research Council pointed out that the particular valley formations along this side of the mountains, running down towards Sylvan Lake and Ponoka, would imply that there had once been a considerable flow that way.'

'Ahuh!'

'It also suggested that the towns along

here could perhaps benefit from a renewal of such a flow. But that's as far as they went. They read no more into it than that.'

'But someone else did.'

'They sure did! Ah, the coffee. Mary, when did I last tell you that you were beautiful?'

'The last time a handsome man stayed overnight with us. Never fails to act as a spur, Ben.'

'I'm just telling Ben about the Fenokee Project.'

Mary groaned and backed for the door with her coffee in her hand.

'That lets me out!'

Seth grinned and turned back to the map.

'Hydro-electric power. That was the answer. And that Senator Roberts saw the possibilities in it. You see, Starling Enterprises – you heard of them, they're big, big contractors in Canada – they tried to sell the Fenokee Project to the government. The idea is to build a dam across here – yeah, I know, some dam! – and construct a series of smaller dams as feeds across these hills here. Don't look so doubtful, the surveys came out like pictures! The big one, the Fenokee Dam, would be the source of God knows how much power. I mean, the dam itself would be over three thousand feet long – almost as long as the Moses-Saunders Powerdam – and it'll make a lake fifteen miles long they say. It'll drop the river's flow through thirty turbines and with an eighty feet head it should develop about eighteen hundred kilowatts of electricity!'

'And that's Fenokee.'

'That's her. Now you'll see that it needed several spillway dams up here in the hills, and a new channel dug from the Icefield to speed up the flow to this river here, and through these valleys, here.'

'Big project.'

'Too big for the government. They got cold feet. Until Roberts stepped in.'

'The American senator? Where did he fit in?'

'He saw the possibilities. They could use the power down there. He suggested that the Americans should be brought in on the Project to supply money and expertise. He guaranteed men and equipment and time schedules if this could be regarded as a joint project. The American firms would be making a packet, or course, but the long-term profit would be Canada's.'

'And it would cement political relation-ships, no doubt.'

'As you say! There were political overtones all right. Anyway, the upshot of the horse trading was that Fenokee would be largely an American financed project, with Ameri-can know-how and equipment, but the spillway dams – and there are four of them

– would be built by Starling Enterprises.'

He grinned suddenly.

'But they bit off more'n they could chew. This all came up seven years ago, you remember, and there was a recession about then, and Starling's were in trouble so – who should be Johnny-on-the-spot?'

'You?'

'Little old Seth Davis! I got the contract, feller, for this dam up here, way above Fenokee. The smallest of the spillway complex, but believe me, there's money, real money in it!'

Ben stared at the map and the thick finger jabbing triumphantly at the paper.

'I didn't realize I was talking to one of the giants of the construction industry.'

'You're not, Ben. Not yet. But when this dam is completed and the books are balanced, I'm going to be in big business. And that'll be just a year from now, maybe less. It's been a long haul, but it's coming home now.'

Ben felt a slight pricking of something that could be described only as envy. In the old days he would have loved to have been involved in a project such as this, and to have been in control, as Seth was, would have been all he desired. But now life was different, he was a different man, with his own business, and a different way of life. Yet the old interests surged inside him as he heard

Seth talk, and he stared hungrily at the map.

Seth Davis was watching him closely.

'When you going back to England?'

'In a couple of days.'

'Why not hang on with us another twenty-four hours?'

'What for – I mean, I'd like to, but I don't want to impose longer than I–'

'Hang on, so you can come up with me, see Fenokee, and take a look at my dam.' There was a strange light in his eyes as he stared at Ben, and the soft smoky brown had been replaced by an excited glitter. He swung around suddenly, calling to Mary, waiting no time for Ben to make up his mind.

'Mary? Bring the bottle in here! Our friend will be staying two nights, not one! And tomorrow we're off early!' He turned back to Ben, grinning.

'To Fenokee!'

3

Ben slept badly. He woke several times before dawn and on each occasion it was with hazy, half-formed ideas on his mind, dark impressions that scored his semi-conscious brain with the dull pain of recall. It was Canada, it was Joanna, it was Pearl and Nebbia and the inquest. And it was

Mary Davis.

When he found Mary alone in the kitchen next morning he had to ask her the question that had crept unheralded into his mind during the early hours. She was standing with her back to him, preparing his breakfast. She spoke over her shoulder.

'Seth's already eaten, Ben, and is out packing some gear in the car. You go on through to the dining-room and I'll pass in your breakfast to you. Two eggs?'

'Yes, thanks. Mary...'

'Ahuh?'

'I ... I didn't mention it last night, but I drove up from Fairmont by way of Fairmont Valley.'

'Oh yes.'

Even those two short words seemed to denote a lack of enthusiasm for the theme of the conversation. But he had to ask her.

'I didn't look around too much, and I took the road to Red Deer at Valley Fork. The police at Fairmont said it was reckoned at the inquest that Joanna must have taken the wrong turning in the snow.'

'That's what we've always guessed.'

'It still seems strange to me, Mary. I mean, Joanna didn't phone to tell you she was coming, and then she drove into Fairmont Valley. Could she have been headed there, rather than to you at Red Deer?'

'I don't see why. Your breakfast is about

ready, Ben.'

'I'll ask you more plainly, Mary. Could she had been going to see someone else?'

'As far as I know she didn't know anyone else around here.'

Ben contemplated her averted head for a moment then in a quiet voice asked the main question.

'Was she meeting someone, do you think? Was she having an affair?'

Mary's back stiffened but she made no attempt to turn and face him. She lifted the eggs out of the pan, pushed them on to a plate beside a mound of bacon, then stood staring at the plate.

'I don't understand.'

'I'm sorry, Mary, but the question was plain enough.'

'I mean I don't understand how you can ask. After all, you knew her as well as I – maybe I should say, better, because you were her husband. Was she the kind of girl who'd be likely to go man-chasing?'

'I didn't suggest that. But you've got to remember, Joanna and I were drifting apart in a sense, the months before she died. We were seeing each other irregularly, and, well, it has occurred to me that maybe she … maybe she met someone else.'

Mary took the plate and handed it to him, but still didn't meet his eyes.

'It was a long time ago, and I think you're

hurting yourself unnecessarily by delving back into it now. Forget it, Ben. Forget it, just hold the warm memories of Joanna, go back to England and enjoy your new life as you deserve to.'

'You haven't answered the question.'

'Haven't I?'

'Not directly.'

'Then I will, since you insist.' A slight edge had crept into her tone and she was looking at him at last. Her eyes were troubled. 'I had no reason to believe that Jo was running around with another man. I have no reason to suspect that she was having an affair. As far as I know there was no one else but you for her. On the other hand, I never asked her, and if Jo was having an affair she never volunteered the information. As for her being in Fairmont Valley, I can only accept the answer given at the inquest. Does that cover all the ramifications of the question that bothers you, Ben?'

'Yes. I'm sorry. I shouldn't have pressed you.'

'No matter.' She turned away, presenting her back to him. There was a strangely defiant set to her shoulders. 'But let me add to what I've said, now you have pressed me. I've told you Jo never said anything to lead me to suspect her. But even if I *had* suspected her, I wouldn't have delved into it. It's not that I'm incurious; it's just that I believe in letting things alone. Once you start turning over stones you can find all sorts of worms.' She gave a short laugh. It contained no amusement. 'She could have been having an affair with Seth and I wouldn't have enquired into it. I'm made that way. I'm the world's original ostrich head; I believe in the security of a hole in the sand. That's one of the reasons why I think you're wrong, dredging all this up now, after seven years. I think you should leave well alone. You've got the opportunity for a life of quiet happiness, the kind I enjoy here. You're crazy to take a chance like this, throwing it aside.'

She stopped speaking abruptly then swung around to face him, her hands on her hips. There were tears in her eyes.

'That was a long speech from me, and maybe it's wrong of me to criticize your conduct. Just because I'm an ostrich head, that's no reason why you should be. Forget what I said.'

She kissed him on the cheek, in the same impulsive manner that she had greeted him yesterday. Then she fussed away to pick up the breakfast plate and thrust it at him.

'Here, get on with your breakfast and stop needling me. I'm never at my best in the morning!'

He was sitting at the table, just finishing the meal, when Mary came through to join him. She poured coffee for them both and cocked her head. Seth was whistling, out of tune, at the car in the driveway.

'Listen to him. A bell in every tooth. Hey, by the way, what I said about Seth and Joanna – there's nothing in that, of course.' She smiled suddenly, at herself. 'At least, not as far as I know!'

4

It was a sixty-mile drive up into the foothills for Seth and Ben and they set out as soon as breakfast was over. Seth told Mary they'd be back for dinner that evening, and then the two men set out in the car along the west road skirting Red Deer. Once they were clear of the town the roads grew quieter, particularly as they began to climb into the foothills. The snow-veined eastern face of the Rockies lifted to the sky ahead of them, and the loneliness of the road they travelled now was emphasized by occasional logging tracks that ran off into the green folds of the forest spanning the slopes. As they drove higher and caught glimpses of the lakes below and the sunflushed parkland above the river valley Seth explained that he was taking the back road up to Fenokee.

'The main highway will be choked with trucks and those damn tourists too. They're beginning to come in droves now that the

Project's all but finished. We'll be quicker this way.'

He talked almost incessantly. Ben said little, but watched the road and the hills and Seth's horny, dark hands gripping the wheel of the car as it jolted along, climbing higher into the foothills. Ben was aware of a certain nervousness in Seth's manner and wondered at the explanation for it; he suspected that it accounted for the ceaseless flow of words, even allowing for the fact that Seth was probably talking about his favourite subject.

''Course, they had plenty trouble down at Fenokee, apart from the problems we had on the spillway. They had to yank the river this way and that, shunt it aside, dry up the bed before they could put in dikes and coffer-dams of steel and earth to widen and deepen the channels. I saw them rip up a quarter-mile chunk of land to full channel depth down there. And then there was Peterson's Bend – they hit some real turbulent waters at that point and before they could get proper soundings to sink dam footings and bridge piers they had to bring in helicopters. They dangled a sounding line with a sixty-pound weight from a hovering chopper and had radio-linked surveyors manning three tran-sits spaced along the shore. The surveyors made simultaneous readings on a marker suspended from the sounding line when the lead touched bottom...'

Ben let him talk. It was interesting enough, and he wanted to see Fenokee, but nevertheless his attention wandered from time to time. What Mary had said to him this morning made sense, but he felt he couldn't just give the whole thing up at this stage. It had proved to be a painful, frustrating exercise so far, and he was getting nowhere. Nevertheless a certain stubbornness of mind made him feel he couldn't leave things this way.

'I was talking to Mary this morning,' he said when Seth at last paused for breath.

'Yeah?'

'She thinks I ought to give up looking into this business, of Joanna's death, I mean. Stop chasing up Pearl's letter, stop looking out this Nebbia character, stop ... turning over stones, I think she said.'

'She's got a point.' Seth's tone was guarded. His hands gripped the steering-wheel firmly as the car lurched and rocked. Ben hesitated before continuing.

'I asked her if she thought maybe Joanna had been having an affair.'

The car jerked and shuddered, Seth swore, and then there was a long silence. Ben had been half-expecting from Seth the reaction he had received from Mary, and when it failed to occur he was disturbed. At last Seth, rather breathlessly, said,

'You asked Mary that? What did she say?'

'That she knew nothing of the possibility.

That she thought it unlikely. Do *you* think it was unlikely, Seth?'

'I hardly knew her.' The words came quickly, a rushing denial. 'I mean, we met several times, and I was around when she called but she was Mary's friend and these hen parties have never been my scene, you know? I usually tried to get out and back to the site, and so on... But if you're asking me, well, no, I don't think Joanna was the type to start running around.'

'So Mary seemed to think. The possibility wasn't raised at the inquest?'

'No. Why should it be?'

'The fact she was in Fairmont Valley.'

'But they explained that. She took the wrong road at Valley Fork. Heck, Ben, I think you're getting bugged with the thing.'

There was an unexpected vehemence in Seth's tone and his jaw was set hard. Ben was surprised, but felt that perhaps both Seth and Mary were right. And yet...

'I don't know. I feel I'd still like to find out what was worrying Joe Pearl. I can't see how I can just pack it in now.'

Seth made no reply. In fact he said nothing for several miles. His earlier rush of conversation seemed to have dried up completely. It wasn't until they crested a long ridge, four miles later, and came out from under the shadowing trees that he spoke again. Then it was only the one word.

'Fenokee.'

It lay before them, arching its gleaming white back to the blue lake it contained. The road ran down from the hill where Seth had stopped the car and skirted the shore of the long artificial lake, slicing past earthworks that scarred the green sward with raw, red-brown wounds, winding among tall trees and through a stand of sequoia, proud and tall, until it reached its long curving finger out to the dam itself, crossed it, and vanished into the woods on the distant side. The dam itself stood high, its face mottled with a series of marching sluice gates that from this distance looked like a line of boxes set into the concrete. Cranes and derricks stood above it, and on the river beyond the dam there were three dredges biting, sucking, plucking at the river-bed, held in place by vertical steel pillars sunk into the river-bed itself. A lighter set out from the nearest dredge as they watched, carrying supplies, and possibly shuttling operators in shifts from shore to dredge and back again.

In the lake itself the water ran blue and deep and peaceful until it reached the gleaming face of the dam where it boiled white in a swift approach to the sluice gates. The height of the damn above the water, and the fact that small capes and islands still appeared in the lake made it obvious that the Fenokee dam was nowhere near capacity yet. There were still treetops to be seen near the lake's edge, half submerged, their peaks riding in the slow drift. Higher up the lake the islands were more numerous but once the spillway dams above were completed, and the waters channelled in full down into the Fenokee they would all disappear, deluged to form the long, wide deep lake that would be Fenokee.

Ben stared and could understand. He could understand Seth's excited interest; understand his enthusiasm. He could understand too the reluctance that the government must have felt, faced with the decision to put the plan into operation, in view of the resources of manpower, equipment, finance and planning involved. And he could marvel at the foresight that must have seen the possibilities in that research report, the possibilities that had led to Fenokee.

'It was the Starling Organization, really,' Seth explained as they turned off the road leading to the dam and began to climb again. 'They put up the project, but the government got cold feet until Roberts sounded off to them. Once he swung in, away it all went. And away I went too, with my spillway project.'

They drove along the narrow road and now they passed two trucks, each bearing Seth's name.

'I'm a million dollars in the red, believe

me,' Seth said with a grin. 'The equipment I got on hire, boy, it'd stretch from here to Montana!'

The road swung dustily through a belt of pine, leaning thick and heavy across the road and sending long arms dipping into the telephone wires gleaming copper in the sun. As the trees thinned the road seemed to open out and they were running up into a narrow valley as the sound of water thundered down to them. At last Ben saw it, gleaming white as its big brother below, Seth Davis's dam, straddling the gorge above them, flanked with thick pine and aspen, banked with derricks and scaffolding, swarmed with red- and green-helmeted workmen.

'That's her,' Seth said with pride and speeded the car towards the small hutted encampment that nestled under the hill beside the dam.

A workman met them as they got out of the car near the main office.

'This is Frank Carson, my chief engineer,' Seth said. 'A good man but weak in the head. You know, Ben, he's been a bachelor for thirty adult years and it's only now that he's finally taking the plunge! Giving it all up for the marital state!'

'But you're making me wait until this dam is finished, Seth. Even though you know I'm attracted to marriage only by what I see with you and Mary.' Carson grinned at Ben, a big man with black eyebrows, dressed in a green shirt and yellow waistcoat of cracked leather, he hardly looked like Ben's idea of a dam engineer, but his handclasp was fierce and his grin friendly. 'Glad to meet you, Mr South.'

'Brought him up to see the dam, Frank.'

'Well I can take over from you, Seth, if you like, because Mr Rose from Starling is up at the office, wants to see you.'

'Rose?'

Seth seemed startled. He turned and glanced towards the office huts and Ben followed his glance. He saw a tall, thin man standing there at the window gazing towards them, waiting. Seth turned back, uncertainly, to Ben.

'I'll go with Frank,' Ben said, and Seth nodded. Something seemed to be troubling him, and there was a furrow of worry between his eyes. He strode off and Ben accompanied Frank Carson along the top of the dam. They walked towards the structure that stood athwart the centre of the dam and Frank led the way up the iron staircase taking them into the glass-fronted control centre in the block. He showed Ben how the control centre worked, powering the sluice gates, and operating the locks.

'We won't be operational for some months yet. To build the main structure of the dam we had to shove the river to one side with cofferdams while we dug for bedrock and built one half of the dam. Once we managed that and constructed this half of the dam – you can see it out here – we sluiced the water through gates in the erected portion and we've now started work on the second half.'

Ben could see what he meant. To the left of the control centre the face of the dam was still incomplete and as he watched he saw the concrete being poured down into the open, steel-strengthened boxes. The river gleamed brown and muddy to the right, sluicing down through the dam, and there was one coffer-dam still remaining on the right bank.

'That's the one to come out today,' Carson explained. 'We'll blast it in about an hour.'

Ben nodded and followed him as he went back down to the top of the dam. He listened while the engineer explained how the channels being cut higher up in the mountains to speed the flow from the Icefield would be finished within six months and how it was important to get the Davis dam completed before that date, so that it could take the speeded flow, and transmit and regulate the waters down into Fenokee some miles below.

'Some deal, eh?'

Seth was rejoining them. He seemed a little pale and he was unable to keep his hands still. Ben wondered whether this had anything to do with his conference with Mr Rose. If Rose worked for Starling Enterprises, who had sub-contracted this dam project to Seth, it could be that Rose had been carrying out a check on progress and wasn't too happy with what he saw. It would certainly have disturbed Seth, if that were the case.

'Your Mr Rose gone?'

'Uh? Yeah, he just drove off down to Fenokee.' Seth seemed to pull himself together. 'All right, Frank, I'll take Ben around now. I think you'll be needed up at the cofferdam. They'll be blowing within the hour.'

Surprise registered itself on the engineer's face and he opened his mouth as though he were about to say something. Ben gained the impression that Carson had expected to accompany them on the tour of the dam and was somewhat put out by what seemed to be a virtual rebuff. He said nothing, however, but nodded to Ben.

'Okay. See you around, Mr South.'

'He's a good man,' Seth muttered as Carson strode away. 'Come on, I'll show you across the dam.'

The top of the dam was some thirty feet wide and at the edge of the wall was an iron guard-rail towards which Seth now led Ben. He seemed constrained and Ben guessed that the interview with Rose must still be on his mind, but he tried to point out to Ben some of the salient points in the construction of the dam. Most of it had already been mentioned by Carson but Ben made no reference to this. The two men strolled along the top of the dam and the sunlight was warm on their heads. Seth pointed to the cofferdam.

'We're blowing that this morning, but if we get along the top here I can show you the construction units we've been using on the main wall.' He hesitated. 'When did you say you were going back to England?'

'I'll be making a start tomorrow.'

'Will we be seeing you again?'

'Not in the near future, Seth. If anything does blow over … over the Pearl letter, and Joanna's death, I might have to come back. I'll certainly look you up if I do.'

'You're going to go on with it, then?'

'I just feel I can't leave it as it is.'

Seth nodded gloomily and stepped across to the guardrail. He peered over.

'Ah, there we are. Come on along a bit farther and you'll see the construction units.'

He led the way to the recently completed upper sections of the dam wall. Just below the rim of the wall were slung a series of two-decked cages, each with deck landings. The decks were sealed by a gate.

'These cages have come in useful. We erected the first stage of the wall and then we used these cages to pull up the dirt tubs, and to transport the men up and down the wall to the bedrock site. They're quite safe; when the cage isn't at the landing the gate stays closed.

As the cage comes up to the landing it pushes this piston, which fires the suspending lever here. The gate runs down, by gravity as it were, and out come the tubs or whatever. When the cage goes down the reverse process takes place; the gate rolls by gravity back in front of the opening. But here, I'll show you. I want to take you down below anyway; there's a lovely honeycomb structure we fill with concrete in the construction that–'

A voice called Seth's name. Seth stared back across the top of the dam. A man in a green helmet stood at the foot of the steps leading to the control house, waving an arm.

'Mr Davis!' His voice came to them thinly. 'Phone – wanted urgently.'

'Hell! Look, I'll be back in a few minutes, Ben, okay? Go on down if you wish – it's a push-button start just there.'

'It's all right. I'll wait until you get back.'

In the event Ben did not. He waited for ten minutes or more, leaning his elbows on the guard-rail, watching the workmen on the far side of the dam, but there was no sign of Seth. He decided to go down by the cage himself. He stepped through the cage doorway, located the button, pressed it and the cage whined into motion. As it sank below the rim of the dam wall the gate came up, as Seth had said, and the cage descended with Ben secured inside on the top deck. He stopped the cage twice on the way down, checking the operation. Each jerking stop caused the cage to rock violently and the gate began to move open but settled again, and Ben was satisfied that everything seemed to be working properly. He sent the cage whining down towards the water gleaming below.

Half-way down the face of the dam he found what Seth had been wanting to show him. Recessed into the wall was a ledge; Ben stopped the cage, the gate was rolled back manually under the pressure of his hands and he stepped out on to the ledge. It was about five feet deep, and he could stand quite comfortably there for it formed an alcove curving above his head. It ran the length of the completed dam face and he was able to walk along, inspecting its honeycomb construction. It was apparently built in units and it would have accounted for Seth's pride for these units obviously meant speed in construction; built off the site they could be transported and slotted into the dam before being sealed in concrete. Even so, Ben felt some doubt about the system. It would be cheap, but he knew what the temperatures could be like up here in the hills and he wondered vaguely whether this type of unit would be able to stand up satisfactorily to the extremes of cold it would be subjected to … still, Seth must have thought of that.

He walked along the length of the ledge

and realized when he came to the sluice gates that the ledge had been constructed for ease of access to the top of the gates, for maintenance work when the level of the dam water fell. At high level the ledge would, of course, be flooded.

He glanced at his watch and then at the distant men working on the cofferdam. Time had been speeding past unnoticed; they'd be blowing the cofferdam within ten minutes or so. He was in no danger where he was but it would be wise to return to the top of the dam to avoid accident. He wondered where Seth was. The phone call must have kept him longer than anticipated. Ben walked back towards the cages at a brisk pace; he'd seen all he wanted to see.

He climbed into the cage and tried to pull the gate shut but it was heavy and he found it difficult to move. No matter; once the cage started the gate would close automatically as he'd already seen when testing the system on the descent to the ledge. Ben glanced up towards the cofferdam once more, leaned out of the cage to check that the rails were free and then he pressed the starting button. It clicked and he thought perhaps he hadn't applied enough pressure. He stepped forward and pressed the button more firmly and above him he heard a heavy traction engine lumber on to the top of the dam.

The cage remained stationary.

Ben pressed the button once more. Nothing happened. He leaned out of the cage and looked upward but all he could see was the blank face of the dam wall. He pressed the button again and again, but there was no response. The cage would not start.

Ben leaned farther out of the cage, clutching the guardrail above the gate. There was no real problem; Seth was bound to come back shortly and once he saw Ben's predicament it would just be a matter of bringing him up. For that matter there were the other cages... Ben glanced across to them. The cage series were linked on the same unit guide-rails and he could conceivably crawl across to the other side, or even walk along the ledge again, but the other cages were all at the top of the dam and there would be no way he could call them down. He glanced at his watch. They'd be blowing the cofferdam soon. There was no real cause for concern, for he was well above the likely waterline; the ledge would only be covered when the spillway was completed and the channel from the Icefield opened but even so he'd be happier if he was up above when the cofferdam was blown. He leaned out of the cage and shouted.

The traction engine was rumbling noisily up above. He shouted again, but realized that it was hopeless. No workman up there would hear his voice against the rumble of the engine. He tried once more, neverthe-less, hoping that a head would appear over the edge of the dam. There was no such response to his call.

He moved back into the cage and pressed the button, jabbing it angrily with his thumb. The whole situation was so stupid, being caught half-way down the dam wall like this. He could think of no reason why the cage should suddenly not respond to its controls. He jabbed repeatedly at the button and glanced at his watch.

It was time for the cofferdam to be blown.

Ben turned and looked back up towards the distant cofferdam. It was clear of work-men, and he had no doubt that the fifteen tons of dynamite that Frank Carson had mentioned to him would now be on the point of being exploded. It was a half-mile distant, the tall steel and banked earth erection, but the blast would hit him here, not seriously, but enough to make the cage swing and dance and shudder. He jabbed the button angrily, there was a sudden whin-ing, a scraping, scratching noise and the cage lurched into motion, the gate rolling shut as it did so. Ben breathed a sigh of relief and leaned back in the cage as it began to inch its way upwards, seeming to move more slowly than it had done previously, but that was possibly his imagination. He suddenly realized that his hands and face were damp, touched by a light sheen of sweat. He'd been more worried that he had been prepared to admit to himself. He looked back towards the cofferdam. A vast silence hung over it, and he realized also that the engine up above him had stopped its roaring. Apart from the whining and creaking of the cage in its slow dragging ascent the whole world seemed to be waiting, breathless, for something to happen.

It came.

He saw the flash, then felt the iron hand pushing and rattling the cage so that it lurched and clanged in its guiderails. Up at the cofferdam he saw the geysers of mud and sand and splintered steel erupting as the blast ripped wide gaps in the structure holding back the waters. He saw the first surge of the river, leaping and driving through the cuts, swelling into a debris-laden torrent that swiftly washed at the rest of the cofferdam and then came racing in an ugly brown and black bow wave, down into the spillway dam. But as the cloud of smoke and dirt rose and thickened and then began to drift in the light breeze the cage stopped its clanging, and began to shudder. Ben looked upwards, grabbing at the stanchions above the gate and craning out. He could see no one up above at the dam wall. The whining of the cage turned to a sudden screeching and it began to slow in its upward grinding movement. Ben cast a swift glance backwards and down and he saw the swift race on the lake surface, the muddy pile of rubble and water advancing down towards the dam wall, a hundred yards, eighty, sixty, and the cage gave a sudden lurch, shuddered and stopped.

But only for a moment. Without warning, as the debris and the black water surged towards the dam wall in a boiling wave ten feet high, the cage dropped breathtakingly downwards, hurtling to the surface of the water, throwing Ben violently against the cage wall, and the gate flew open for Ben to slide uncontrollably through the opening. He was scrabbling at the stanchions when the cage lurched again, and stopped as though punched by an iron hand, but his grip on the stanchion was broken. Next moment the water thundered in.

CHAPTER 4

1

It crashed into the cage like a sledgehammer. Sprawled on his side and grabbing at the sliding gate, Ben was half-protected from the immediate force of the floodwater by the wall of the cage but even so it lifted him and threw him across the cage, breaking his grip yet again, and driving all the breath from his body as he was slammed against the far wall. The cage swung wildly and Ben was half-blinded as mud and dirt and debris swirled in chokingly about him. His arm was now lodged between the stanchion above the gate and the wall and it saved him for there was a sudden washback as the floodwater, striking the dam wall, was thrown back. The wash surged over him and the cage swung again; something struck him in the mouth and grazed his cheek, a piece of driftwood was flung against the stanchion and cut his hand and then a second, subsidiary wave was rushing into the cage, more turbulent, less forceful than the first smashing blow, but twisting and surging as it met and fought with the backwash from the wall. Ben was lifted bodily again and was hanging out of the cage now, but his wrist was still caught between gate and stanchion as he swung helplessly. He was swallowing filthy water and he was blind with spray and mud and he choked, fighting for breath as the rushing sound of the water seemed to get louder and louder in his ears until it was no longer the thunder of water but the slow pounding of blood. Everything was hazy and distant, there was a deep pain in his chest and he was unable to move his arms while his buffeted body began to ache with a long delicious slipping feeling that seemed to reach the length of his body until it found sharp, needlepoint purchase in his skull, to explode into kaleidoscopic, whirling colours and lights. Fingers of pain beat a tattoo against his heaving chest, he was retching and his face was in the swirling water while a great drumming began way above him, in the distance, where the sky and the clouds lay. He shook his head like a punch-drunk boxer attempting to rise and the pain engulfed him again, briefly, before he felt the sweet surge of air into his lungs, sharp and incisive, a clean knife driving into his chest. He lifted his head and his vision blurred, then cleared momentarily.

He was lying on the floor of the tilted, half-wrecked cage, his upper body resting against the broken gate, his wrist trapped in the twisted metal. His legs dangled helplessly outside the cage, pulled in the swirling water which, even as he looked about him with lungs gasping for air, swept in again, less violently, but still seeking the wall as the beat of the waves induced by the blowing of the cofferdam pushed it again and again. The water swept over him once more and the cage lurched, dropping him lower in the water, so that he took another great mouthful and lifted his head, spluttering crazily. A litter of greasy filth and wood and mud rushed around him and poured out of the cage again, only to splash back as it hit the wall, and he fought for breath. He looked up, pulling on his trapped arm to clear his head from the water and he could see the blue sky.

Next moment, distantly, he heard the voices.

His wrist was numb but his arm was pressed against the wrecked gate and a moment later he felt the shuddering that was communicated through the metal. He tried to swing his free arm across in an attempt to pull himself farther into the damaged cage but he could obtain no purchase. The shuddering increased, and now it was clearly a man's voice he could hear. A man's voice, a name he recognized. His own.

'South! South! – hang on, we're coming!'

The surging of the water had settled to a rough but uneven battering of the cage. It lifted him, pulled at him, but he was aware of no pain now, nor of cold, for he was only half-conscious, and drifting in a mental haze. Even so he struggled to keep his head above the washing surge, and scrabbled with his feet for the wall, to prevent his legs getting crushed between cage and bars. Dimly he could discern movement just above him and he could hear the creak and whining snarl of metal in movement. The slow realization came through to him that one of the other cages was coming down, and rescue was near.

He felt the cage lurch and settle lower in

the water. He could raise himself no more and the movement pushed his head under the surface, but something wound itself firmly and fiercely into his hair and jerked his head up. Fingers, a man's fingers; the lurching had been caused by a man jumping on to the top of the cage, and now the man was lying on its roof, leaning over, reaching down to pull Ben's head clear of the choking water. Ben's eyes cleared and he found himself staring mindlessly into the contorted face of Frank Carson. Carson was mouthing something but the words themselves were not communicated to Ben above the rushing noise in his ears. The cage lurched again as boots landed heavily on it and someone else was swinging himself over the edge to brace himself against the top of the gate and get an arm around and underneath Ben's body. A third man arrived and Ben's senses began to clear momentarily; they were standing either side of him, one holding him, lifting him towards Carson as the third man gently freed his twisted wrist from its trap between gate and stanchion. He was aware of the curious sensation of being airborne, lifted bodily, and then everything was sideslipping into darkness.

Not a complete darkness, but a raging, throbbing darkness that swung him this way and that until his balance was lost and he was a twisting, space-bound animal, disorientated, lost in air. A tickle began in his fingers and turned slowly into a violent, thrusting tingle; blood coursing through his veins, bringing life back into his numbed arm. The voices were louder and clearer but they were incomprehensible in their shouting and then he was aware of hands on his body and he opened his eyes.

A stretcher. He was on a stretcher, and there above him loomed the control centre, rapidly giving way to the roof of an ambulance. He saw a face he knew, Seth's face, twisted and shuddering with an uncontrollable and fearful anxiety and then there was a clanging noise, a dim light and a drifting into a darkness that was, this time, complete.

The male nurse was called Charlie Chevrotier and he had Indian blood and a great smiling face. He patted Ben's cheek in mock affection and turned to Seth and Frank Carson.

'He's gonna be all right. Couple days rest, go easy with that arm, and there'll be no long-term worries at all.'

'That's not the way it feels to me right now,' Ben objected, growling in his chest.

'Aw, you got multiple bruises, a lip thick as a rare steak, a scratch down your cheek, your hand is a bit lacerated, your wrist is broken and your arm damn near pulled out of its socket but otherwise there ain't a damn thing wrong with you! Quit bellyachin'!'

Frank Carson was grinning.

'One of these days, Charlie, you're going to end up in this place and half the camp is going to be gathered around your bed tellin' you how well you ought to be feeling!'

'Never see the day, Frank! I'm a patcher who don't get patched by no crummy male nurse like Charlie Chevrotier! If I ever get hammered up here I'll bawl long and loud for a doctor and I'll whop anyone who tries to come near me with anythin' I can lay hands on! I know the dangers, feller!'

'Thanks for telling me,' Ben said and tried to ease himself up into a sitting position.

'Go easy!' Charlie assisted him in the movement, until Ben was sitting upright, with his legs over the edge of the bed. Seth stood in front of him, with concern written all over his face.

'Seriously, Ben, how're you feeling?'

'I'm all right, I think. Damn sore, though. I've been awake about an hour, talking to Charlie here – whom I've got to thank for setting my wrist, I gather. What the hell happened though, that's another matter.'

Frank Carson's head bobbed forward.

'I went up to the firing and saw they were all clear so I was making my way back to the dam, with about two minutes to go to firing when I saw the cage, with you inside it. I belted the car down to the dam, hoping to phone through to stop the firing but I didn't make it in time. The blast came, the cage dropped and there you were in the water!'

'I have you to thank for saving me.'

'That blasted gate and stanchion saved you! If you hadn't got snarled up there you'd have been battered unconscious against the wall and down you'd have gone. No, once I saw you were trapped it was just a matter of getting men down in the next cage and scrambling across to lift you clear. But you were damned lucky!'

'Unlucky, would have been my word! And it could have been two of us down there. What happened exactly, Seth?'

Seth Davis appeared distinctly uncomfortable. He shrugged, obviously feeling most awkward about his part in the accident. He coloured slightly.

'Well, I took that call, and that took me a good twenty minutes. I looked out and saw you'd gone down alone but I thought that was okay – I wouldn't bother to join you. Then I had to call a heavy engine across to move some materials from the other side of the dam and I got involved with that. I thought you could be left to yourself. Time went faster than I realized. I did come back at one point and look over the edge for you but you must have been along the ledge somewhere. I didn't see you, anyway, so I left you to it, and walked back to the control centre. Then, when I realized the blast was imminent and you weren't back up I started for the cage to see what was happening. I saw it begin to come up, then it stopped again. Just before I got to it, down it plummeted, and the waves came in. Frank was on hand almost at once and he was over into the next cage while I called up Charlie and the ambulance. It was a close call, Ben.'

'You don't need to dwell on that!'

'God, Mary'll give me hell!'

'It wasn't your fault, don't worry about it, Seth.'

As he spoke, Ben glanced at Carson and saw that the chief engineer was staring at Seth with a strange, slightly puzzled expression on his face. He seemed about to say something, but kept his counsel as Seth hurried on.

'We'd better get you back home, anyway, and you'd better stay with us a few days longer. Frank, can you get the car around?'

'You ain't asked me whether he's fit to travel yet,' Charlie stated in an aggrieved tone. 'He is, but I'd appreciate bein' asked. And Mr South, don't worry about that wrist too much – get it X-rayed in town, but I think it won't be much more'n a hairline fracture. You was movin' it all right when you were out to the wide.'

'God save me from quacks and Charlie Chevrotier,' Carson said and stamped aggressively out of the hut.

Charlie grinned and winked at Ben.

'He's jus' sore because when he told me he was gettin' married I diagnosed wind in the stomach and offered him an Alka-Seltzer. Some fellers you can never satisfy. They got no faith in the medical profession!'

2

Charlie Chevrotier's diagnosis relating to Ben's wrist proved to be right. There was no real break of any seriousness in the wrist; it was a hairline fracture that demanded a plaster cast for five or six weeks but nothing more serious than that. When the Davises pressed him to stay on for a while Ben was able to say, therefore, that he was quite fit to travel and he took his leave of them. Before he did go he heard Mary tell Seth what she thought of him for exposing Ben to such a danger but though it finally degenerated to a good-natured banter between the three of them something odd had crept into their relationship. Ben was unable to explain it, but Seth seemed too jovial in his company, excessively good-humoured in a strained manner. He put it down to the fact that Seth was embarrassed by the accident.

'The suspension pin had sheared through,' Seth explained. 'When the cage was half-way up the dam wall it must have snapped away and down you went, lickety-split.'

He was at a loss to explain away the failure of the starting-button, however, and this plainly upset him, so that finally Ben pressed him no more on it, suggesting to Seth that perhaps it was due to a faulty supply. It yet lay at the back of Ben's mind that it was strange that the cage should be faulty in two respects.

Mary seemed genuinely sad when he finally took his leave. She kissed him and pressed his hands.

'Now we have met and got to know you, Ben, don't leave it another seven years. And next time, why not bring a new wife with you?'

But that was something else again. As the jet took him back to England Ben was still considering the situation, for basically it hadn't changed. His trip to Canada, his nine days away from the office, had in no sense allowed him to reorient himself. No problems had been solved, no decisions reached, no mysteries cleared. He still had no idea why Ellen Pearl had written to him, no idea based on factual evidence, that is. All he had was the suspicion that Joe Pearl had to some extent delivered perjured evidence at the inquest, but Ben could not imagine what had been changed from the truth, and why. To that was added Dr Nebbia's conduct –

which to the outsider could be explained away but which still left Ben with the feeling that this was one more suspicious circumstance. And then there was the fact that Joanna had gone into Fairmont Valley at all, and had not phoned Mary Davis to say that she was on her way to see her.

It all added up to the fact that Joanna was still on his mind, still very much with him. The shadow was still there and he was unable to let go of the problems that niggled at him. Seth and Mary had suggested that he should; they could be right, but he couldn't let go. Stubbornness, or a feeling that he owed it to his dead wife or to himself ... his motives were hazy and difficult to categorize.

All he did know was that he had to go on with it.

It was what he told Pete the first day he got back to the office. He wasn't inclined to talk about it at first for Pete had obviously been busy while Ben had been away and Ben joined him in conference with the representative of the equipment hiring firm he had contacted. They haggled prices most of the morning and argued about schedules and break clauses in the contract but the upshot of it all was that Henley and South Ltd agreed to hire a considerable amount of earthmoving equipment for the Cornelius Hotel contract.

There was no break for lunch that day; it

was a working lunch with Sir John Emsley and the two other nominees who would be joining the board. Emsley was a sharp little man with birdlike eyes and a habit of pulling at his left ear whenever he wanted to break in on the conversation, but he was a shrewd man and he knew what he wanted.

Nor was he without a sense of humour.

'I'm glad we've managed to reach agreement,' he said as he replaced papers in his briefcase. 'I must admit that I'd hoped for more than a twenty-five per cent share in the business, and I'd seen myself more in the role of Financial Controller than Joint Financial Director with you, Mr South but, well, it's not a bad bargain, I agree. I'm sure I will be able to reach agreement with my colleagues and yourselves – we'll raise the financial backing necessary for expansion while you put in your skill, expertise and present company assets. All very amicably agreed. Though it would seem that not all your business discussions end the same way, Mr South.'

He was looking at Ben's wrist and hand.

'I've expressly avoided asking him about it,' Pete said, gesturing to the waiter for the check. 'But I bet the other feller got off worse, hey, Ben?'

They all laughed, the waiter arrived with the check, Emsley and his colleagues left and Ben waited while Pete signed the check.

They decided to walk back from the restaurant to the office and Pete lumbered along beside Ben, glancing at him quizzically.

'Well, I've not asked till now but how *did* you get trussed like that?'

'It was an accident.'

Ben explained what had happened and Pete listened in silence, shaking his head slightly. When Ben had finished he opened his mouth to speak but Ben beat him to it.

'All right, Pete, don't say it! I know – it's hardly consonant with my image of the respectable English businessman, scrambling up and down the wall of a dam and getting immersed in filthy water after an explosion.'

Pete laughed, creasing his heavy face with pleasure.

'I've never been of the opinion that you'd make a respectable businessman, and somehow the image of you on that dam wall isn't too much out of character, as far as I'm concerned. I bet you really enjoyed that visit – up until the accident, anyway!'

'You could be right.'

Pete hesitated, then waited until they had crossed the street before he spoke again. His voice was now edged with care, as though he was aware he might be treading sands that might slip away from him.

'And the trip, overall?'

'Did I enjoy it?' Ben looked at Pete but the older man avoided his glance. 'How can you enjoy anything that you can't finish?'

'You didn't make out then.'

'I didn't make any sense out of the whole thing. I'm no further forward ... in fact, maybe things are worse.'

'So it's not finished.'

'No.' Ben explained briefly what had occurred in Canada, about Ellen Pearl, and the way every avenue seemed to close to him as he went on. Pete sensed his frustration.

'Not much you can do about it from here, Ben.'

'That's right. And I'm needed here, with the Cornelius contract rising up in front of us, and the other contracts to complete. I can't stay in Canada to follow the thing through. So, I decided to use an enquiry agent.'

'The hell you did!' Pete stopped and stared at Ben in surprise. 'You've engaged a private detective? This I've got to hear about!'

Ben told him.

He had reached the decision while he was in Vancouver. His mounting dissatisfaction, his frustration, his refusal to let the thing go had culminated in the decision to find an agent to look into the matter more thoroughly than he could do. He'd found Vince Rider.

He had liked what he saw in the man. Rider was not above middle height, and he was slimly built but there was the springy hardness of thinly coiled steel in his bearing, his handshake was firm and positive and his eyes were sharp. He had an air of cool confidence and Ben felt that the man knew his job; an assertive independence was quickly revealed as one of his qualities.

'It'll be a month, maybe longer, before I could handle anything for you, Mr South. Right now I'm up to my neck in a fraud case and that'll take all my time. I have two assistants but...'

Ben hadn't wanted assistants. He'd wanted Rider because he felt that the man would be able to produce results. And wouldn't flinch from telling Ben truths that hurt, if it came to that.

Ben gave him the file he'd prepared.

Rider looked at the file's contents briefly and his eyes flickered up to Ben's as he realized that the details appertained to the man facing him. He closed the file gently.

'I think I'd like to have it first in words, from you, Mr South.'

Ben nodded, thought for a moment to decide where to begin and then went back to the time he moved to Edmonton with Joanna. He spoke without emotion, and with little expression in his tone. Rider listened carefully, his brown, washed-out eyes never leaving Ben's face. When the surveyor finished his story Rider nodded and sat in silent contemplation, staring at the floor.

After a while Ben rose and walked to the window, looking out with his hands clasped behind his back. The account he had given Rider had left him feeling depressed and nervy; it was not pleasant, asking a private enquiry agent to look into the interstices of his own life. He heard Rider stir in the chair.

'You have your hand in plaster. What happened?'

Ben explained briefly, and was a little nettled when Rider pressed him for further details. 'I don't see it as relevant,' he complained.

'You're peevish, Mr South. I'm just enquiring after your health.' Rider hesitated. 'Why don't you see it as important?'

'Do you?'

'Heck, I don't know. Not yet anyway. But at this stage I'm just groping around for facts. It seems to me that when I start on this I've got to go talk to this Pearl character first, to see if there's anything more he can dig up about his old man. You say he's prepared to help; that'll be a welcome change! Then there's this retired policeman Durrance – a trip to Shelby on expenses, it could be worse. I look into your Dr Nebbia again, do some general sniffin', and I chase up this Seth and Mary Davis up at–'

'I'd rather you didn't involve them.'

'How do you mean?'

'They've told me all they know, and I've

115

put it in the file. Don't bother them, Rider. They're friends.'

Rider ran a doubtful finger along his long nose, and eyed Ben, frowning.

'I'd really like to talk things over with them.'

'I don't think it's necessary.'

'Because they didn't want you to go on with the enquiry, is that it? You don't want them bothered?'

'They didn't think I should proceed, that's true, but–'

'What about that dam, then?'

A silence fell between them. Ben was uncomfortable, and he felt as though a subconscious warning was sounding for the second time though he could recall no first occasion.

'What do you mean?'

Rider shrugged his slim shoulders and stood up.

'I just asked a question. I'm coming cold to this whole thing, I don't know a thing about the Davis couple–'

'They're nice people.'

'Yeah, but I don't know them and I just see facts you've given me. You seem to have shrugged off the dam incident, but the cause of the accident wasn't explained satisfactorily, was it? Seth Davis didn't want you to press on with your enquiries and then you near get killed. Me, I'm just a suspicious dick, but I'd like to talk to Davis and his wife.'

'I think you're off beam. I don't want them distressed.'

Rider's face had remained blank.

'As you say. Well, anyway, I can't handle your case for a month at least. If you can wait for my services, fine, I'm your man.'

'I've waited seven years. A few weeks won't harm.'

But it left Ben restless. When he told Pete about Rider, Pete had said little but he had an honest face that cloaked feelings very badly. Ben knew that Pete thought the continuance of the investigation was a mistake. It would be an opening of old scars, knives cutting into half-healed wounds. But Pete was older and softer and less direct than Ben and he was unable to come right out and tell Ben he was making a mistake. Seth and Mary Davis had said it but Pete felt that it was all too personal for his interference.

Even though it could affect Henley and South Ltd.

Ben buckled down to the routine work at the office and on the sites, but his mind still clung to the spinning questions in Canada. And at last he knew there was one thing he could do, at least; there was the man Durrance, the officer who had left the Fairmont police department and gone to Shelby, Montana. There was the outside chance that he wouldn't blow his top the way Captain

McGregor had at the suggestion that a police witness might have committed perjury. There was the chance that Durrance could clear the matter entirely, make Rider's intervention unnecessary. He'd been involved, he'd been on the spot.

Ben spent a week-end trying to trace the man by transatlantic telephone and late on Sunday afternoon finally managed to obtain an address which could be that of Sam Durrance, late of Fairmont. He was listed in the telephone directory in Shelby, but there was no reply from his phone. Ben drafted a letter to the man, explaining his situation and asking for any advice or assistance Durrance could give him in the matter. The same evening he wrote to Billy Pearl, telling him that he suspected his father's 'shame' might in some way have been connected with his services for the police department, but he in no way specified what the action might have been. He requested that Billy be kind enough to assist in further enquiries that might be made at a later date. Then, it was a matter of waiting. And brooding.

3

September came and drifted into October. Ben saw the successful completion of one building contract and the first draft of the

118

company formation agreement was laid on his desk. Pete told him that the solicitors were now waiting on the details of the Cornelius Hotel contract and he and Ben paid several visits to the site. October slid quietly into November. There was no word from Rider and Ben received no reply from Sam Durrance of Shelby, Montana. On the fifteenth of the month a letter arrived from Canada. It was from Billy Pearl.

'Dear Mr South,

Thank you for yours. I have the whole garage to take care of now and I can only begin to understand how bad things were. I'm just glad that the old man had the sense to put a bit of money aside in the bank, that wasn't for touching. It looks as though I'll have to be touching it, sure thing. Business is bad.

Sure, I'll help in any way I can. I don't reckon there's a deal I can do to help out but count on me. I reckon that it's a kind of duty, since it was Ma's letter which brought you out here in the first place. She's home now, but she don't look good. She don't move, nor speak, just sits there in the chair, following me with her eyes. Let me know when you want any assistance.

Yrs truly,
Billy Pearl.'

The letter had been written with care, on thin

airmail paper, but at the bottom was a less legible scrawling, obviously done in a hurry. Ben read it with difficulty. 'The old lady just passed away. This sure is a bad business.'

Ben returned the letter to its envelope. So the old lady had died. And he was no further on in his investigations. He wondered whether he would ever discover what really happened that time at Fairmont Valley. Everyone concerned with the inquest seemed to be dead, or simply uncommunicative. He wondered also what had happened to Rider.

He received the answer next morning. It was in the form of a cable.

'South – Am making start, Shelby, Montana. Rider.'

The cryptic words unsettled Ben. When he had met Rider in Vancouver, some of the questions Rider had posed were unpleasant and most unwelcome. Seth and Mary Davis were Ben's friends – and they had been Joanna's friends too. It was inconceivable that they would have anything further to add to the account that they had already furnished Ben. As for the cage at the dam, that had been an accident, it could have involved Seth for that matter...

But it hadn't.

Yet when Ben had come back up, supported by Frank Carson's friendly arms, he had seen the fearful anxiety in Seth's eyes, anxiety for a friend who had come close to death. Or for a friend who had not come close *enough* to death.

Rider's insinuations had soured his mind, and Ben was angry. But he hoped Rider would produce the answers, and soon.

CHAPTER 5

1

The police officer shifted his wad of gum from one cheek to another, pushed his cap back to scratch among the thick hair just above his left ear, scowled at the pass that Rider had showed him and grunted.

'You back, then.'

'Seems so.'

'And you got the captain's permission too.'

'That's right.'

'Persistent, ain't yuh?' The office lumbered grudgingly to his feet and turned to take the keys down from the wall behind the desk. 'You a private dick, I s'pose.'

'Suppose away.'

'Don't get funny with me, feller.'

Rider made no reply and the glowering officer mumbled to himself and walked towards the door leading to the cells. He jerked a finger contemptuously at Rider.

'Come on down this way, and you can see your client like you planned.'

Rider walked quickly after him, not deigning to deny that the man in jail was his client, and followed the burly officer down the corridor to the cells. The last cell in the block was occupied; the others were empty. The officer stopped at the occupied cell, unlocked it and swung the door open to allow Rider entry. He spoke to the occupant of the cell.

'You been complainin' that things've been quiet since the Saturday crowd left yesterday, Sam. Well, we allus aim to oblige. I brought you some company.'

Sam Durrance raised his head to stare at Rider as the slim man entered the cell. The door clanged behind the enquiry agent and the officer said, 'Holler out when you're through,' before he walked away. Rider stared at Sam Durrance. He saw a broad-shouldered man whose build would once have been described as powerful but which had now run to ugly fat. He was about fifty-five, his iron-grey hair was cropped close at the sides but lank and dirty on top of his head, and the eyes that stared unwinkingly at Rider were small and mean, lodged in deep pouches and shadowed by a ridged brow. Durrance was wearing a shirt, denim trousers and shoes; the shirt was open to the waist and his belly spilled over the waistband on his trousers. He was rubbing the bare flesh of his stomach, his fingers kneading, the thick knuckles digging into the heavy, dark-haired paunch.

'I don' know you.'

His voice was deep and his tone surly. Rider was aware that Durrance in no way welcomed an interview.

'I've come a long way to see you, Durrance.'

'You could've picked a better time. I got gut trouble. This lousy jail.'

'You're due out in five days' time, I hear.'

'Why you so interested?'

'I'm interested in you, Durrance. I wanted the chance to talk to you, ask a few questions.'

'I don't answer questions.'

'Wait until you know what they are.'

'Go to hell. That broad had what was comin' to her an' if she thinks she can send some snoop in here to get me to give her enough rope to hang myself she can think again! If she wants to file suit on me, brother, just tell her that what I'll have to say in court will make even the judge blush. I can tell him all about the way she been carryin' on over at Sioux Falls in the spring, I can tell him a heap, enough to get her run right outa Shelby for importunin', at least. She's not dealin' with a mutt, you tell her that. I know what's what. I didn't spend twenty years in a police department without gettin' to know all about whores like her. If she–'

'That's what I want to talk to you about.'

'Whaddya mean?'

'Your twenty years in the Fairmont police department.'

The piggy eyes twinkled suspiciously at Rider.

'You mean you ain't come on that whore's sayso? What the hell's going on?'

'My visit's got nothing to do with the charge that landed you in here. I just want to talk to you about the time you lived up at Fairmont.'

Sam Durrance straightened up from the stool on which he was sitting and helped his belly back into the confinement of his waistband. He was taller than Rider had realized. He shook his arms like a boxer loosening up, turned and walked to the back of the cell to pick up a mug into which he poured some water from an enamel jug. He drank the water, grimacing. Rider waited patiently. Durrance turned at last, leaned his back against the wall and regarded Rider with care.

'Okay, you want to talk about Fairmont.'

'I want to ask you about your time in the department there.'

'Long time ago.'

'Five years.'

'You been workin' on me.'

124

'You left Fairmont and came down here five years ago. Why did you retire so suddenly?'

'None of your damned business. But no harm in you knowin'. I got framed on a drunk charge, on duty, and there was talk of my pension being reduced so I told 'em to stuff it where it hurts most, and I upped and got out of there.' A swaggering note had entered his voice. 'Some principles a man gotta stick by.'

'So you retired to Shelby. Why Shelby?'

'Why not?'

Durrance grinned unpleasantly and Rider guessed that the policeman was going to enjoy a little playing of the line, with Rider hooked at the other end. This way Rider wouldn't be getting far. He decided to go straight to the point.

'Two years, or so, before you left the Fairmont force you had occasion to go up into Fairmont Valley, as investigating officer in a car accident.'

'You tell me.'

'You were accompanied by two other officers and you found the car wrecked among some trees. The driver you found in the snow, some distance from the vehicle. She was dead. You later gave evidence at the inquest. I'd like you to tell me about it all.'

'You seem to know all about it. Can't say I recall it as well as you do, feller. Seems to me you got more of the detail than I have. Long time, you know.'

'Her name was South. You'd have remembered that, not a usual name.'

'Yeah. Yeah... You a Canadian, ain't you? You'll be tied up with that feller who wrote me from England, couple of months back.'

'You didn't reply to him.'

'Thass a fact. Nothin' to say.'

'Because you don't remember the incident?'

'Because I got nothin' to say.'

'Why?'

'Whaddya mean, why?'

'A man's got reasons for keeping quiet about something he's done in the course of his duty. Reasons, maybe such as that he's ashamed of what he's done, or he's scared–

Durrance came up from the wall belligerently, and took a step towards Rider, who didn't move.

'Hold your horses, feller. What you tryin' to say?' When Rider remained silent Durrance glowered at him. 'You dicks are all the same. If I was in uniform now I'd work you over good, you dam' smart-alec private dick! You try to say I was scared of somethin', huh, I put bigger fellows than you behind bars when they was shovin' knives under my nose! Scared! I got nothin' to be scared of–'

'And shame isn't an emotion you suffer from,' Rider sneered. For a moment he thought the deliberate taunt might cause Durrance to lose his temper and perhaps say more than he wanted to, but although the man's face became suffused with blood he maintained control of himself. There was a short silence, and then Durrance said,

'This feller South. What's he want?'

'Information.'

'About the way his wife died?'

'That's right.'

'It's in the transcript of the inquest.'

'I'd like your version of it.'

'Accidental death. Like the coroner said. So why's this guy sniffin' around, what's he pushin' you out here for?'

Rider paused, eyeing Durrance coolly. He wasn't sure how many cards he should play.

'Well, let's say that my client, Mr South, has some reason to doubt the official account of the circumstances of death.'

Something flickered deep in Durrance's piggy eyes but his features remained without expression. He was in control of himself, and Rider suddenly realized that this man was more than just a mindless, dirty mound of flesh.

'You'll have to spell that out more clearly.'

'I don't intend to. Beyond saying we think a man might have perjured himself.'

'You tryin' to say–' Durrance caught himself, and smiled grimly. 'No. Why should any witness perjure himself? Joe Pearl had local respect, and he was the only witness bar me.'

'And Dr Nebbia.'

'Doctors is respectable.'

'That leaves you.'

'Police officers is respectable too.'

'But they can lie. Did you lie at the inquest, Sam?'

Durrance regarded him coldly.

'I had nothin' to lie about. You better shove off now, Mr Private Dick. Before I lose my cool.'

'Joe Pearl lied, didn't he? What about you, Sam? Did you fool the coroner too?'

Durrance said one word, an obscenity, and lounged back against the wall. Rider stared at him for a while then glanced around the cell disgustedly and walked back to the door to shout for the police officer to let him out. While he waited for the man to shuffle through with the keys a silence fell. It was broken by Durrance.

'Hey. This South feller – the dead woman's husband. If there was information, would he pay for it?'

'Is there any information?'

'Would he pay for it?' There was a gleam in the mean, angry eyes that stared at Rider. Before the enquiry agent could answer, however, Durrance walked across to his stool abruptly, sitting down and muttering fiercely and excitedly, 'Not enough, though, not dam' enough!'

He refused to answer any further questions from Rider. After the door clanged to behind him Rider said to the police officer escorting him.

'Friendly feller, Durrance.'

'He's all right.' The man chuckled. 'Give you a roustin' hey? I tell you, man, even an ex-cop can't get a dislike of private dicks out of his gullet.' The thought that Durrance had proved unco-operative seemed to put him in a good humour, however, and make him more inclined to suffer Rider's presence longer. 'You wanna cup of coffee before you leave us?'

Rider accepted the offer and the police officer obtained two paper cups of scalding coffee from a machine installed in the corridor outside his office. He handed one to Rider.

'Real coffee this, not like your Canadian mud.'

'So they tell me. Look, this Durrance, what's he been doing in Shelby since he got here?'

'Aw, Sam got in at Shelby about five years ago, and set up with a small liquor store top of Victoria Hill. Didn't do so good though, mainly 'cause he was drinkin' most of the profits, an' once that was gone he took to drinkin' his capital too.' The man shook his head. 'Hey, Sam had some real ring-a-ding-dings up on the Hill.'

'He had to close the store down?'

'That's it. Ran out of cash and got to the state where he had to sell up. That was three years ago. He did a bit of gumshoin', you know, dirty stuff like you private dicks get up to, divorces and that sort of malarky, but he was already past it, you know? Couldn't stay sober, or wouldn't. Then he took up with Mandy Court–' He sighed expressively and rolled his eyes.

'That's why he's in here now?'

'They had a ruckus last month, and he put her in hospital with a broken arm and facial injuries. He got just thirty days because it was either him or her if ya know what I mean. She was flourishin' a bottle. Aw, they'll be back again, maybe, if she waits long enough till he gets out. Talk is she's got some feller over at the railroad right now. Who knows? That broad, she ain't better'n a whore.'

'And Sam?'

'Aw, his trouble is the last year he's just been broke. If he's got drinkin' money, he's all right.'

Rider finished his coffee and stood up, nodding his thanks.

'Well,' he said, 'Durrance might seem all right to you but he's not my idea of a bosom pal.'

'Sam's all right,' insisted the officer, and as Rider walked out through the door he added sourly, 'leastways, he don' go pokin' his nose into other people's business!'

130

2

The unsatisfactory nature of the Durrance interview was communicated to Ben over the transatlantic telephone and it seemed to confirm for Ben the fact that he was wasting his time. This was the first interview Rider had conducted on the case and he was now going to try to speak to Nebbia and Billy Pearl again. Ben thought there was little to be gained from either but this was Rider's job now and he respected the agent's ability to turn over stones. Rider was an experienced investigator; he might yet discover something worthwhile. He certainly left Ben with the impression that Durrance had had something to hide, something he knew concerning Joanna's death, something he might yet sell. But Ben wasn't in the market, not yet. It was all too vague – suspicious, but suspicion wasn't enough. He wanted more before he could take positive action.

Not that he could see what positive action could be taken. The whole thing was seven years old.

And his friendship with Pete Henley was six years old but Ben couldn't behave positively in that either. Since he'd returned from Canada something had happened to their relationship. It was as though Pete felt shut out by the personal nature of Ben's problems; he was a bear of a man, but he was sensitive and he didn't press Ben in any way, about the Cornelius situation, the outstanding contracts, his business worries – or about Joanna. The two men continued to work amicably together, they laughed and joked but it was surface stuff. Something was missing; they both held back. It was a curious experience that neither man could have categorized but they seemed to be treading warily, like two embarrassed people at a cocktail party, both aware they were not strangers, but circling each other, unwilling to take the first step back to a natural friendship, wary in case it proved to be a false step.

He heard nothing more from Rider for two weeks. He made no attempt to communicate with the enquiry agent for he knew that Rider would contact him as soon as anything important arose. He plodded on doggedly with his work at the office, even though he continually found his mind drifting back to Canada, and Joanna was often in his thoughts.

It was for this reason that when he was sitting alone at his flat one evening Ben suddenly turned up the sound on the television set. He had been sitting there with a whisky in his hand, not really following the play he had been starting at, and thinking about Joanna, and Fairmont Valley, and Rider working for him out there, when suddenly the name of the man on the screen caught his attention.

He had seen the programme in question on occasions; it was a series called, simply enough, *Giants*. It consisted of an interviewer called Tom Hale discussing each week the rise of some industrial or commercial 'giant', and putting questions to the man concerned, sometimes in filmed interviews, sometimes face to face in the studio. This evening Tom Hale's face flashed on the screen against a background of cranes and derricks, and he announced the 'giant' for the week, the man who would be talking about himself and his business empire.

The man was Grant Starling.

He sat in the fibreglass chair in the studio, a massive crag of a man, his heavy jaw clamped hard, deep lines running down his cheeks, his hands gripping the arms of the chair. He was at ease yet he communicated a sense of power even when relaxed, and there was a luminous quality about his eyes, a piercing quality about his glance, that the television lighting was unable to subdue. He sat squarely and uncompromisingly as though this attitude must base his every action and thought, and he stared unsmilingly at Tom Hale as the interviewer began his brief account of the rise of Starling Enterprises. Hale, a young man who sometimes irritated Ben by a certain brashness of manner in his television appearances, was swinging his chair to face Starling more fully.

'Well, Mr Starling, so much for the emergence of your engineering and construction firm. You've gone from strength to strength, you've become one of the giants of the construction industry in Canada, what is it that now brings you to England?'

Grant Starling's voice was as craggy as his appearance. He shrugged a massive shoulder.

'I would have thought it was common knowledge. I've decided to realize a life's ambition. I want to own a newspaper.'

'So many – if I may use the word – tycoons seem to want to move into the newspaper business! Why is that, Mr Starling?'

'I can't speak for other ... ah ... tycoons, as you put it. Me, it's just something I've always wanted to do.'

'Do you see it as philanthropic? I mean, the saving of a newspaper such as the one you're negotiating for?'

'I'm not out to save anything. I'm a businessman. I'll buy it if they'll sell, and if I think I can make money out of it.'

'Ha, ha, I'm sure that you're underrating yourself and your intentions! After all, what about the Starling Foundation? Surely–'

'You mean the Philip Starling Foundation.'

'Yes, surely that is philanthropy in its–'

'There were motives other than pure

philanthropy behind it. Taxation was one; a memorial was another.'

Ben smiled faintly. Tom Hale was obviously sent a little off balance; the answers were coming too quickly, and too directly for his liking. Moreover, he seemed a little unsure about Grant Starling's attitude. In Hale's experience men who established educational foundations were only too keen to claim the highest motives for so doing; this man disclaimed such motives. Or at the least, relegated them to a position behind other more personal ones. Hale's reaction was to wander more widely, but Grant Starling showed a certain impatience in his replies to some of the inane questions that were asked. Ben leaned forward; it was interesting, wondering just how this unscripted interview was going to go. Hale was becoming somewhat nettled and Ben remembered at least two occasions when, similarly out of favour with the man he was speaking to, Hale had turned to the attack, with effect. It made good, if unfair to the victim, television. There was the possibility now that Hale was moving that way.

'Well, we'll leave that point there, Mr Starling, shall we? Let's turn to politics. Have you ever thought of becoming a political animal yourself?'

'Never.'

'Is that because you consider the real

power lies in big business?'

'I've not thought of it in that way. I like the business world. I don't think I'd like politics, where a man has to say, sometimes, what he doesn't believe.'

'But you don't object to *using* politicians. I mean, you'll have done your fair share of lobbying in your time.'

'I've put my point of view to politicians and to the Press, yes.'

'Have you ever gone further?'

'I don't know what you mean.'

'Well, have you ever found it necessary to, shall we say, financially support a man's running for political office?'

'I've never found it necessary.'

'Perhaps because you've been able to get what you want by using less obvious methods of persuasion?'

Grant Starling hesitated. He was staring curiously at Tom Hale.

'I don't know what you're driving at, Mr Hale. I think it would be a good idea if you explained what you mean by that statement, or otherwise move off on another tack.'

It was a strangely gentle approach for such a forthright man, but Ben could see that Starling was plainly telling Hale that he'd better be careful with his choice of phrase. Ben was inclined to agree, also; the way Hale was heading there was the possibility of a dogfight with perhaps a libel action based on an innuendo. Hale was smiling.

'I'd prefer to decide my own tacks, with respect to you, Mr Starling. And explain what I mean? Well, it's difficult, for these things are so often under cover and never see the light of day. Politics and business these days go hand in glove. And we regularly see examples where the hand is ... grubby, shall I say? We have an example in the United States right now, don't we?'

'I don't know what you're referring to.'

'Surely you do! It's been well publicized. I refer to the congressional enquiry that has been instituted to look into the affairs of Senator Joseph Roberts. You've been aware of it, surely.'

'I have.'

'No comment to make?'

'None. I let the Americans get on with their own affairs. I don't presume to interfere, or comment. Not my business.'

'What isn't your business?'

'Eh?'

'You mean the Roberts enquiry isn't your business?'

Starling's jaw was now rock hard, and his eyes were cold. Hale was still smiling, but it was the smile of a tiger.

'You do surprise me, Mr Starling. I would have thought you'd take special interest in the Roberts enquiry. Certainly, were a congressional enquiry mounted to look into the affairs of one of my associates I–'

'What did you say?'

'I don't know – did I imply that Senator Roberts was an associate of yours? A slip of the tongue, I assure you. But he is being investigated, and you *have* had dealings with him, haven't you?'

Grant Starling was leaning forward slightly now. His voice was level and unemotional and yet there was a hint of menace in its very quietness.

'Explain yourself more fully, Mr Hale.'

The nervousness of Hale's smile was now apparent but the man had gone too far to back down completely. He tried to bluff out the menace.

'I'm saying that the enquiry in the States is looking into the senator's business dealings. I'm saying that you have had business dealings with the senator. That's all. I'm not implying–'

'You're not implying that my business dealings are the subject of the enquiry. You'd better not be doing that, Mr Hale. Because if you are you're in trouble. I've had no dealings with the senator.'

'What about the Fenokee Project?' Hale was swift to come back in, a little angrily. Starling remained cold.

'I've had no dealings with the senator. The Fenokee Project was a contract I won from the government. The senator had dealings with the government also. He had no dealings with me.'

'But you've met him!'

'I've met you too, Mr Hale.' Starling smiled grimly. 'And I've formed impressions about both personalities.'

For a brief moment Hale was at a loss for words. Then he forced a laugh, produced an inanity about first impressions and all being fair in love and television interviews, and turned to the Fenokee Project itself, in an attempt to deal with facts where he could not stumble into dangerous argument. Ben listened while Starling talked about Fenokee, pointing out it was largely an American financed project, and that Starling Enterprises' main interest was in the spillway dams. A short clip of film was shown, illustrating work on the site. It kept Ben watching; it was interesting to realize how the work had speeded up since the film was taken.

When the programme ended Ben was left with the definite impression that Grant Starling was a man to be reckoned with, and for once Tom Hale had more than met his match.

The next day he found himself thinking several times of the interview, and of Grant Starling, and he remembered the broad splendid sweep of Fenokee as he had seen it that morning with Seth Davis. But then Starling was pushed to the back of his mind as the more urgent matters of the office and contracts supervision forced themselves upon him, and he spent days down at the sites, discussing progress reports with site foremen, poring over plans with Pete Henley, meeting Sir John Emsley and the other men who were to become directors of the newly formed company. And the time slipped past. Until Rider placed a person-to-person call with him.

3

Ben took the call in his office. While he waited for it to come through he twisted nervously in his chair. His hands were wet with perspiration. As soon as the phone rang he grabbed for it, to hear the operator ask if he was Mr Ben South. Moments later there was a crackling sound and then Rider's voice, remarkably clear over the line.

'Mr South? This is going to cost you, I know, but I thought you'd want results as soon as I got them. I'll mail you a written report as well. As it happens, I'm speaking from London, not over the transatlantic line – I had to be over here for a few days on an extradition matter. Anyway–'

'What did you get?'

'No holiday, that's for sure! And it was becoming damn cold when I left. As for results, well, I got them, and yet again I didn't get them.'

'You'll have to explain that to me.'

'I'll try, Mr South, but it's not easy. The thing is, I seem to be working on hunches and that's dangerous. It's too easy to convince yourself that you're right when you work like that, convince yourself when in fact you're barking up the wrong tree entirely.'

'Try convincing me.'

'Trouble is, there's little evidence, and if you want me to speak with honesty it may be that you're too involved personally to be able to evaluate it anyway. However, let's start at the beginning.'

There was a brief moment of hesitation as though the enquiry agent were clearing his thoughts, then his voice came again, crackling over the line.

'First, I saw Durrance. I already told you there was no dice there, although I'm pretty sure he's got something to give us, but he's too slimy for my liking. Then I went to see Billy Pearl and had a long talk with him. I like him, sad little feller, business going downhill, but honest and prepared to do all he can to help. But he can't do much. Those papers you mentioned to me, they just ain't around.'

'What do you mean?'

'The whole shed outside there went up in a blaze a couple of weeks back. Accident, it seems, but not a thing left. So there's no

141

help from there, even though he's keen to assist you, says he feels kinda responsible...'

Ben remembered all the junk in the shed and closed his eyes. A fire, destroying all Joe Pearl's possessions, all the papers he had hoarded. Somehow it seemed as though another door had closed. Rider's voice continued, its Canadian inflection emphasized by the telephone.

'I spent a long time chasing around Fairmont and Red Deer and ended up at the local newspaper offices. I got friendly with the editor of the *Courier* and we had a few beers together–'

'Do you make a practice of befriending newspapermen?'

'We've got a lot in common. Long noses and longer memories, just for a start. Anyway, it didn't turn out to be completely unproductive. Then...' Again Rider hesitated. 'Then I went to see Seth and Mary Davis.'

Ben gripped the receiver tightly. A coldness that he was unable to explain ran through his veins.

'I wanted you to leave them alone.'

'I'm sorry, Mr South, but you ask me to do a job, I got to do it the way I see it. Asking me to stay away from those two people inhibited me; I needed to see them, talk to them.'

'They are friends.'

'That's as may be. To me they're sources of information.'

'I'd already spoken to them. They'd given me all they knew.'

'So you told me.'

'What do you mean by that?'

'Don't get too excited over this, Mr South. You just have to realize that there are times when people don't ask the right questions because they're asking them of friends; sometimes not the right questions, sometimes the right questions but the wrong way of asking.'

'Are you trying to tell me Seth and Mary knew something that they kept back from me?'

'Well, not exactly, maybe it wasn't deliberate, or perhaps it was. I don't know!'

'You're not making sense!'

'I knew this was going to be difficult!'

'You're making it so, with veiled accusations!'

'But that's the trouble! It's like I told you, Mr South, I'm low on proof but jammed to the eyeballs with theories! And I don't damn well know whether they're crazy theories based on innocent coincidences or not!'

Ben sat back in his chair and glared coldly at the wall. He was beginning to think it had been a mistake asking the enquiry agent to act for him in Canada at all. He was angry with Rider even though he recognized that the anger was a little illogical. It made no difference.

'You'd better let me have the theories and the coincidences, and let me judge. After all,' he added with heavy sarcasm, 'I'm the one involved, as you said.'

'Hear me out before you really get worked up, Mr South! And remember, like I told you before, I'm coming cold to this with no preconceived ideas about facts or people! Right, now what did I have after a week out there? Let me put it this way. First, a dead woman, whose death was described as accidental. Second, Joe Pearl and his conscience, communicated vaguely through his widow, now dead. The third fact we have is the uncommunicative Dr Nebbia–'

'What did he have to say?'

'Like you, I didn't get to first base. Fourthly, there's Sam Durrance, also remarkably uncommunicative. Let's just take these facts alone. The only link these people have with your wife is the inquest, and none of them are able, or concerned, to talk about it. Blank wall.'

'But you worked out a theory about it.'

'Not quite. I was just curious. I cerebrated, I looked at these characters and asked myself what else they had in common, apart from having given evidence at the inquest. And I saw it.'

'I don't.'

'None of them were living in Fairmont.'

'So?'

'So they all moved from Fairmont after your wife died – at intervals over two years, true, but they moved, Durrance to Shelby, Pearl to Waterton Park, Nebbia, well just a few miles north, outside the city limits but–

'I see no significance in that.'

'I didn't at first. But they more than just moved. What was Joe Pearl? A mechanic of sorts, employed by a local firm. When he moved he started up his own garage.'

'He won some money on the horses.'

'That's what he told his wife. What did he tell her before he died? And Nebbia, what was he? A doctor with a small practice, undertaking police work for a fee – until a little while after the inquest, when he moves north of the town and opens his own nursing home. Did he play the horses too?'

'And Durrance went to Montana two years later–'

'To drink his way through a liquor store, lock, stock, barrel and bottle.'

'I think I'm beginning to see the glimmer of your theory.'

'I thought you would. Simple enough, after all, if you sit back and look at things. They give evidence, they move out, they do what they've always wanted to do, go into business on their own account. Where did the money come from? Joe Pearl maybe worried about it, after he'd done it and was near to death. Was he given the money, as

145

the price to keep quiet, or worse, to make a statement that wasn't true?'

'Perjury.'

'Nasty word. But that's our problem. A beautiful theory but no proof. Circumstantial evidence of a kind, unsupported by hard proof. It could all be shrugged off as coincidence.'

'And would be in a court of law.'

'Ahuh. Besides, if that theory holds up it leaves two major questions unanswered. If those three fellers did give false evidence at the inquest–'

'Why did they do it, and who paid them to perjure themselves?'

'Exactly. We're stuck at that point. Think of the "ifs". *If* they perjured themselves, *if* they were paid to so act. We've no proof at all about either. Now if we could find out a reason, and a person...'

Ben had been listening hard; he suddenly realized that anger had seeped away as Rider had talked to him. He was in a more rational mood now.

'You've got more theories than that.'

'That's right. I got to that point and I said to myself *suppose* there was something not quite *right* about your wife's death. Something had to be hushed. That needs money. It was provided. Well, I got around to seeing my editor friend then. Who's got the cash around here, I asked. He told me where it all was. Up in Fairmont Valley, he said, that's where the money is.'

'And that's where Joanna died.'

'That's it. But there was one problem. Who would she be friendly with in Fairmont Valley? How could she get to know anyone up there, assuming it wasn't an old friend? Seemed to me only two people could tell me. So I went to see them.'

'Seth and Mary.' Ben hesitated, thinking. 'I'm sorry, Rider. You were right. You had to see them and ask them. You couldn't know they wouldn't be able to help you.'

There was no reply immediately and Ben felt a shiver at the back of his neck.

'All right. Let's have it,' he said quietly.

'They had nothing to tell me, as you said. They couldn't help. They had no idea who she might have known up in Fairmont Valley. This is where the trouble starts, Mr South, and I'm sorry, but I wasn't happy about it all. I went back to my newspaper friend. I checked on everyone who lived up in that valley, names, background, and couldn't see any connection.'

He paused.

'Things don't come logically, but they come in the end. You got to remember, a local paper lives on local news and when newcomers arrive they get a bit of publicity, not much, but enough. Particularly if their names are, well, not unfamiliar nationally.

147

There was one character who did live in the valley for a while, about the relevant time. The paper had a few shots of him. One of them showed him living it up in a local club. I took a look at it, and I recognized one of his companions. It was a friend of yours.'

Ben hesitated before he made his guess.

'Seth Davis.'

'Ahuh. Now let's be reasonable and not jump to conclusions, but let's look at the facts too. Your wife visited Mary Davis. Your wife was found dead in Fairmont Valley. This feller in the photograph has or had a rented house in the valley. He's been shot here in Seth Davis's company. So what? Okay, I did some more digging, because this by itself isn't much. How well did Seth know this character? I found they met in college, were in the same year, whopped it up some. And when he comes to Fairmont they meet again and get around a while together. The big question is, how far did this connection affect your wife? The answer, we can't tell.'

'But you can theorize.'

'Guess, is better. There's the *chance*, Mr South, that Seth introduced your wife to this feller; there's the *chance* that she drove into Fairmont Valley to see him; there's the *chance* that this man paid the witnesses for silence about something – maybe they could in some way connect him with her, I don't know. But there's the *chance* that he didn't want it known she'd been seeing him, didn't want to get involved in an inquest. And paid for silence.'

'But why the hell, if that's the case, why the hell didn't Seth mention it to me?'

'I didn't ask him, but I kept on guessing.'

'What could the reason be?'

'You haven't asked me the name of the man in that photograph.'

'All right, damn you, what's his name?'

'Philip Starling. Grant Starling's son.'

CHAPTER 6

1

The room was silent and yet it pounded and drummed for Ben. It was a moment before he realized that the sound was in his own head, that his heart hammered against his ribs, and he was aware of a series of wildly flashing images in his brain, Seth, Mary Davis, the dam, the craggy man on television, the dwarf pines above Fairmont Valley, the winding river where Joanna had died. He tried to speak but his mouth was dry. The phone crackled in his hand.

'A while back, Mr South, I said that the

three witnesses at the inquest had something in common. They came into money. I didn't add that Seth Davis seems to fall into a similar situation. You asked me why he said nothing to you about young Starling knowing your wife. One answer could be that he didn't, because she never met him and I'm theorizing a lot of nonsense. But what if they did meet, and what if Starling did pay off the three witnesses? Why *then* didn't Seth mention the meeting? Because he got paid off too.'

'The spillway dam.'

'That could be the size of it. I checked, you know. Seth Davis wasn't a big operator before your wife died. He had a successful firm, certainly, but it wasn't a high flyer. All right, he's local, he's on the spot when the Fenokee Project is mooted, but why does he get the spillway dam project?'

Ben was thinking furiously and angrily. Rider could be right, but there could be a rational explanation too.

'He could have put in a low tender.'

'Maybe. I thought of that. I thought maybe his tender was the lowest. No real way of checking. But I tried. I learned who else had tendered for that dam and I went to see them. Normally I don't think I'd have got much help, but one of the contractors concerned has always been sore about that contract. He reckoned that the Davis tender

150

wasn't the lowest. More than that, he said that in his opinion it wasn't adequately costed, even suggested that corners had been cut in construction strengths. He wouldn't divulge where he got his information from, probably the construction grapevine, I don't know, but he reckoned that the Davis tender should never have won through.'

'But if Seth and Philip Starling were at college together, if they were friends...'

'That's right. Maybe Davis got the Starling contract because he was old buddies with Starling. It could be right. But Starling Enterprises is big. It's in business to make money. Does the old pals act make sense in business? I don't know. My reaction is that it doesn't, not where it's a question of sentiment as against profit. Davis wasn't big – but he will be after he finishes this dam.'

'You're trying to say–'

'No. I'll say it. There's the *chance* that Seth Davis was paid, too. For his silence. Then, and now.'

'I can't believe it. Mary was Joanna's friend. Seth–'

'All right, you can't believe it. Maybe you shouldn't anyway, because there's very little of it that I can prove. Hell, we're dealing in suppositions. We can't prove that Starling knew your wife, we can't prove that Davis got the contract as payment for keeping his mouth shut, we can't prove a connection between Starling and Durrance, or Nebbia, or Joe Pearl. It's all pure guesswork. All we know is that these characters flourished after she died, and that Davis knew Starling. And apart from all that we still haven't been able to suggest the answer to the big question.'

'What question?'

'*If* all these payments were made, *why* were they made?'

Ben's hands were still wet. He was beginning to wish he had never started this, never paid any attention to Ellen Pearl's letter, never gone to Canada, never met Mary and Seth in the flesh, for now he was confused, he was suspicious, he was angry and he was bitter. Maybe he should have left it alone as Seth and Mary had said...

'The dam.'

'What?'

'The dam,' Ben repeated dully. 'The accident at the dam. Seth told me he thought I ought to leave Joanna's death alone. So did Mary, she said it too. Then Seth took me to the dam. And I almost got killed.'

Rider cleared his throat.

'Look, I may have started that suspicion in your mind before I left for Canada. We better not get started on that, Mr South. Remember, we're dealing in possibilities, and we can't prove any of them. It's just hot air. Forget the accident at the dam.'

'You implied that it might not have been

an accident.'

'That's so, but–'

'Seth could have been trying to stop me looking into the matter further.'

'I think you should leave it.'

'Everyone keeps telling me that! Everyone keeps telling me to leave the damn thing alone! Why? Why the hell should I? I wanted to know how my wife died! Now it seems as though I may have to ask *why* she died! And why I almost did too!'

'We don't know that she died other than from natural causes,' Rider said stiffly.

'No, but don't tell me that there isn't that other *possibility* that's come into your mind!'

'All right, it has occurred to me, but there's a coroner's inquest which says different!'

'If we can prove the links between Starling and Davis and the witnesses things could look different.'

'Slim chance, the way things seem to be turning out. I can't see how we can pressure them. If you want my advice, pack it in. We can't take it further. It's a dead-end.'

'The hell it is! Why didn't you check on the dam incident, for instance?'

'How could I?' Rider's voice was getting angry. 'To start with you tell me to stay away from Davis–'

'An instruction you disregarded!'

'All right, what the hell do you want? I did the job as I saw it should be done! That meant checking with Davis and his wife! It did not involve checking on your accident at the dam!'

'Why not?'

'If I went pussyfooting around up there asking questions I'd get nothing from anyone to start with, and then I'd only be putting Davis on his guard anyway! And if he is guilty of trying to kill you I'd still like to know *why*, first, before I go charging up around that spillway! I've no desire to end at the bottom of the river myself!'

Ben took a deep breath, expelled it slowly and sat back. After a moment he managed a wry smile. His voice was quieter.

'Maybe I needed that.'

'I know what you mean. Fact is, it's so damn frustrating. We're up against a brick wall, a wall of silence, my friend. We shouldn't let it bug us.'

'No. All right, we'll take it calmly. I'll tell you what we'll do. We'll–'

'My advice is to drop it, Mr South.'

'Why?'

'Two reasons. First is that you're up against the big battalions. There's an awful lot of money in Starling Enterprises, and if our guesses are right and some money has already been invested in keeping these people quiet, there'll be plenty more to follow it.'

'That's no argument. If I can face this man Philip Starling with what we have I might be

154

able to–'

'You didn't let me finish. That's the second reason. You can't face him.'

'Why not?'

'Philip Starling died in an air crash, just eighteen months ago.'

2

It was more than likely that Rider had been right. It was more than likely that Ben was adopting the wrong course in attempting to take the matter further. But he was irritated when Pete first asked him what news he'd received from Rider, and then had agreed with Rider's remark that Ben should leave things alone.

'I don't see it's any of your damn business, Pete.'

Pete Henley made no reply immediately. Then he shrugged despondently and sat down, his heavy face fixed with an impassivity that masked the hurt Ben knew he felt.

'All right,' Pete said. 'I was wrong to stick my nose in, asking you in the first place. But don't say none of this is my affair.'

Ben knew what he was feeling and there seemed to be no reply he could make. Pete leaned forward earnestly.

'I can't stand back out of this, Ben, because we're tied, not just by the business we run but by friendship too. All right, it's got a bit bruised just recently and I don't quite know why, but that still raises no reason why I shouldn't speak out. I thought it was right you should go out to Canada to get Joanna out of your system. But you didn't get rid of the old memories; instead you've become obsessed with it all, until it seems as though it's ruling your life. You're up against a dead-end but you're still kicking, and I just don't see the point.'

'Pete, I've got to know. I've got to know what happened out there and why it had to be hushed up. Grant Starling is in this country and I intend asking him about it.'

'I think it's a mistake.'

Pete said no more about it; he'd made his point. But it soured the atmosphere between them and angered Ben even though he knew in his heart that Pete also had some rights in the matter for Ben was unable to concentrate upon the business. And that affected Pete. Nevertheless Ben was determined to see Grant Starling. The trouble was he proved elusive and difficult to contact. A female voice over the telephone finally made an appointment for him, with a member of the Starling entourage, when Ben stressed the urgency and importance of his reasons, and he arranged to travel up to London two days later.

Grant Starling had a suite of rooms at a

London hotel and Ben was ushered up. When he entered the second of the rooms he half-expected to see Starling himself, but he was met by a tall smiling man who extended his hand politely.

'Mr South? My name is Rose, Edward Rose.'

The name was familiar but it took Ben a moment to remember where he had heard it before – then he remembered that Rose had been checking at Seth Davis's dam the morning Ben had gone there. Rose had left before Davis rejoined him for the tour of the dam. He looked at the man now as he was waved to a chair. Rose was thin, well-dressed, hollow-cheeked. His eyes were deep set but sharp as a bookkeeper's, his hands sensitive but strong and he had an air of serious sophistication. He sat down behind a mahogany desk, linked his fingers together and smiled. He had good teeth.

'Well, Mr South, I understand you have something important to discuss.'

'Yes. With Grant Starling.'

'Perhaps you'd like to tell me about it.'

'No. I'm sorry, but I need to see Starling.'

The deep-set eyes regarded him seriously. Rose nodded.

'I appreciate that you regard your visit as of importance. You must appreciate also that Mr Starling is rather a busy man. Perhaps it would help if you were made aware of my situation. I am Financial Director to Starling Enterprises, and this trip I'm acting as a sort of personal aide to Grant Starling. I'm acting as a sort of filter, you understand? Now normally you wouldn't even get within a mile of me, let alone Grant, but I gather from the communication you had with my secretary that your business is of a personal nature. It may be that it's important, so I decided to see you. But Grant, he's a busy man, an important man, with a great deal on his mind. While I would hesitate to place your business in the category of trivia, I'm afraid I need to know the purpose of your visit, in case it does amount to something which Mr Starling should not be bothered with.'

'I assure you it's important.'

'I'm sorry, South, but assurances are not enough. I must know what it is you wish to discuss.'

'It's personal.'

'To Mr Starling?'

'Yes.'

Rose leaned forward, spreading his hands wide in front of him. He looked sad.

'In that case I must insist even more strongly that you tell me what it is about. You will understand, South, that Mr Starling cannot be concerned with trifling matters relating to what people regard as personal and important. It's my job this trip to protect him from people who want handouts, or who want assistance, or wish to presume upon chance acquaintance–'

'None of these applies to me.'

'Oh, I'm sure, but it's more than my job is worth to allow you to go in to see him on the basis of what you've told me so far. I need to *know*, Mr South.'

Ben hesitated; he wasn't sure how much he should tell this man, how much he should keep back.

'It's about his son.'

'Philip?'

Rose's eyebrows were raised enquiringly. He waited.

'I want to know if he knew my wife,' Ben said quietly.

'I'm sorry, but is there any reason why he should have known her? And what does this have to do with Mr Starling?'

'My wife is dead. She died in Fairmont Valley. Philip Starling rented a house in Fairmont Valley. I want to know if he was acquainted with my wife.'

Rose was frowning.

'You have grounds for supposing he did?'

'I want to see Grant Starling about it.'

'I don't see how he can help you.'

'That's for me to decide.'

'No. I must protect Mr Starling. You'll have to tell me more. I can't expose him to something I know nothing about.'

'All right! I want to know if Philip Starling

159

knew my wife; I want to know if she was visiting him before she died; I want to know if the fact of her visit was hushed up by Philip Starling – and if that's the case, I want to know why!'

Rose folded his arms and sat up very straight. He looked like a schoolmaster, stern-visaged, about to reprove a small child.

'You say you want to know these things. You think Grant Starling can provide the answers? I doubt it.'

'Let me find out.'

Rose stared at him for several seconds, deep in thought. At last he rose and walked across to the window to stare down at the busy London street. His back was to Ben when he spoke, in a quiet musing tone.

'You know, Grant Starling has come a long way in forty years. He's sixty now, but still tough as teak. Except in one respect. Like everyone he has what has been called an Achilles' heel. And you, Mr South, will be touching that particular vulnerable spot.'

He swung away from the window and came back to the desk, to perch on its edge and stare at Ben.

'The little you've told me so far doesn't make things very clear in my mind, but it does leave an impression with me. The impression is one of evasion, of dishonesty, of hiding the truth – and these are charges you would seem to be levelling against

Philip Starling. Am I right?'

'They're charges I *could* be levelling, but am not necessarily doing so.'

'You speak with a certain caution. I think that caution should be extended to all your conduct from now on. You would be extremely unwise to take this any further.'

'That's a phrase I've heard before.'

'And disregarded, I take it. All right, why should you listen to a warning which is not supported by reason? Let me try to give you the reason. You've heard of the Philip Starling Foundation? Yes, most people have. If you saw the appearance of my employer on television recently you'd have heard him deny that the Foundation was established through pure philanthropy. That's true. It was a foundation established through sentiment – as a memorial to Philip Starling, his beloved son. You do know, of course, that Philip died about eighteen months ago.'

'I do. That's why I find it necessary to see Grant Starling himself, rather than his son.'

'And that's why I counsel caution. Let me be frank, South. How old are you? Thirty-six ... a year older than Philip would have been now. Philip's mother died when he was ten, and from that point onwards Grant Starling took over his education and his training. Philip was to inherit the empire that Grant was building, and Grant tried to ensure that Philip came out of a school tough enough to make him face the responsibility. So he rode his son, rode him hard, made him fight for his pleasures, and struggle for his experiences. It wasn't an easy road that he mapped out for his son, and Philip found it tough going. But he kept going, and maybe he'd have become the man his father was, and still is. He never had the chance.'

He paused, glancing involuntarily towards the door behind him.

'I'm not going to say that Philip didn't have his faults, his weaknesses. Some people saw them – I did, for one. His father saw no faults, recognized none, accepted none. He drove Philip on the road to power and success in business and he saw no weakness and would admit to none. In other words, South, I'm telling you that Grant Starling worshipped his son.'

'I don't see that this has anything to do with me.'

'That's where you're wrong. I'll be frank. Philip Starling may well have had feet of clay; he may well have strayed from the path his father beat out for him; he may well have lived it up somewhat on occasions – indeed, I know of a few times when he did just that. This isn't to support any of your theories about your wife, you understand, but just to warn you – for though Philip may have been less than the businessman of steel his father wanted to make him, his father never saw

162

this side of him. In a sense he blinded himself to it, in a sense it was kept from him. Now if you go in there and raise with him the questions you've raised with me, two things will happen. He'll disbelieve you, and then he'll get angry. On the first count you'll have gained nothing; on the second, you could be in trouble.'

'What do you mean, trouble?'

'This is no threat. It's just a fact of life. Grant Starling is not a vindictive man, normally. But you attack his son, and you attack him, in the most personal way you can. Do that, and he'll hit back at you, as hard as he can. And believe me he can hit harder than any man you've ever known.'

He stood up away from the desk and towered over Ben.

'The decision is yours, of course. But my advice is, go home, forget this, and leave Grant Starling alone.'

Ben shook his head.

'I can't do that.'

Edward Rose said no more. He contemplated Ben for a moment with his steely book-keeping eyes, as though puzzled by the obduracy of an entry that wouldn't balance, and then he walked to the door behind him, tapped lightly on it and entered. Ben waited, and a few minutes later the door opened and Rose stood framed in the doorway, tall and gaunt.

'Mr Starling will see you now,' he announced formally. Ben entered the room and Rose left it, closing the door quietly behind him. Grant Starling rose from behind his desk and stared at Ben. He was even craggier than he had appeared during his television interview; there was a hard, whipcord leanness about him that gave the impression of a life lived out of doors rather than in the boardroom and for all that he was sixty years old he looked capable of a hard day's manual labour alongside the men who worked for him on his construction sites. He had been wearing glasses to read – a concession to age that he obviously despised, for he removed them as he got up from his chair and cast them contemptuously on top of his papers – but his glance was piercing in its summary weighing up of the man he observed. He seemed not displeased by what he saw. He grunted and stuck out a hard-knuckled hand.

Starling waved him to a seat.

'I don't know you, Mr South.'

'No. We haven't met.'

'You'll excuse me if I ask you to come straight to the point, but my stay in England will not be a long one, and I've a great deal to do. I understand you've been insistent in wanting to see me. Here I am.'

'I want to ask you about your son.'

'Philip? You knew him?'

'I never met him.'

Grant Starling frowned, offered Ben a cigar from a box on the desk, and when it was refused took one himself and bit off the end, thoughtfully. He flicked on a table lighter, and leaned forward to light the cigar, but his eyes remained fixed on Ben.

'Okay, what do you want to ask about him? You're a surveyor, I understand.'

'That's right. But my visit has nothing to do with my profession. This is a personal matter.'

'You said you didn't know Philip.'

'That's right. But perhaps my wife did.'

Starling was leaning forward, his elbows placed on the desk. He drew on the cigar, his glance unwavering as he contemplated his visitor; there was no change in his expression but a certain steeliness had crept into his bearing.

'Perhaps your wife knew Philip. Go on.'

'Seven years ago your son rented a home, a lodge in Fairmont Valley.'

'Up near Fenokee. Could be.'

'Not could be. He did.'

'Have it your way.'

'My wife was living in Edmonton then, but she visited friends in Red Deer from time to time. I believe she might have met your son–'

'You *believe* she *might* have met him?'

Doggedly, Ben ignored the sarcastic interruption.

165

'–and might have visited him at the lodge in the Valley. I have reason to believe she might have been visiting him the night she died.'

He paused, watching Grant Starling's face. It was granite-hard, and the cigar was held stiffly between rigid fingers. He said nothing, however, and Ben continued after a momentary hesitation.

'While driving down through the valley she skidded and the car plunged down over the bank and into some trees. She must have been dazed; according to the inquest she staggered around for a while before she lay down in the snow. They found her two days later. Now what I want to know–'

'Yeah. Tell me.'

'I want to know whether your son tried to hush up his connection with my wife, by bribing witnesses at the inquest. And if he did, why he found it necessary to so act.'

Starling drew on his cigar impassively.

'You can prove this, what you been telling me?'

'No. Not prove, exactly. But–'

'What is this, a shakedown?' Starling's voice was gravelly and he rose suddenly, thrusting the cigar towards Ben in a stabbing gesture. 'What you trying to pull?'

Ben rose to his feet also.

'This is no shakedown, Starling, I just want to get at the truth!'

'Don't make me laugh! What is this story

you come shovin' at me? You trying to make out my son was fooling with your wife? Seven years ago? When nothing is proved, but you suddenly decide, after all this time, that you want to get at the truth? What's the trouble, feller, business not so good? Listen to me, I'm not the man who's interested in supporting impecunious surveyors with charitable handouts! You've come to the wrong guy!'

'You don't understand–'

'I understand fine, Mr South! I know a shakedown when I see one! You think you can come around here with some veiled hints about the way my son was carrying on with your wife, throw in a hint of perjury and some other crimes as well maybe, nothing proved of course, and you think that I'll be so scared, afraid some mud might stick to my son's name that I'll pay up to shut your face! Well, all I can say is you've come to the wrong man, feller! I earned all I got, and I don't pay out on a shakedown like this!'

'Let me tell you the rest of it!'

'To hell with the rest of it! I've heard all I want to and more than I need to!'

'What's the matter? You afraid to hear what may be the real truth about your precious son?'

It was a stupid taunt, born of frustration and anger and Ben regretted it as soon as it passed his lips. But regret was useless; Grant

Starling threw the cigar to the carpet with an angry gesture and raised a clenched fist, one finger shooting out in a vicious warning gesture towards Ben.

'Let me put you straight, South! I don't shake down, and I don't stand for muck-raking. You come in here with *mights* and *believes* and use hints that suggest you can smirch my boy's name. Well, let me say this. I've broken bigger fools than you, bigger men than you, and I can snap you into little pieces too. And I will if you follow this rubbish through. There's nothing you can tell me about my son, no *real truths*. I brought that boy up myself, I trained him, I made him the man he was turning into. And he wasn't becoming the sort of man you're implying he was! You heard the way he died? He was on a flight from Vancouver in a private plane. Just the two of them – Philip and the pilot. They crashed into some low hills, made a belly-landing. Philip was thrown clear, he could have got the hell out of there. But he didn't; he went back to try to drag the pilot clear. And while he was doing that the petrol tanks went up. He was burned to death. You hear that, South? He was burned to death when he could have got clear! So don't come to me with the sort of smear you've got. I won't listen to it, I don't have to listen to it, I don't believe it, because I knew Philip! I knew him for what he was, what I made of him! And if you try to say any more, try to spread this smear outside this office, I'll break your back personally, after I've made you eat your words!'

'Don't threaten me, Starling!'

'Why the hell not? You think I can't take it through? You think I'm not big enough to see you put under? Don't try me, South; it'll be your funeral!'

'I mean to get at the truth!'

'The only truth is what I've just given you! Take this further and I'll break you!'

Starling was in a towering rage. His voice had risen until he was shouting and his fists were clenched, half lifted at his sides. The lines on his face were etched deep, emphasizing the hard jut of his jaw as he glared furiously at Ben. The surveyor heard a slight movement behind him and half-turned his head. Rose had re-entered the room, obviously hearing the raised voices.

'I think you'd better leave now, Mr South,' he said in a quiet, level voice. Ben stared bitterly into Grant Starling's eyes.

'You won't listen because you don't want to listen! You're afraid of what you might hear! But don't think you can scare me off, old man! I don't scare easily!'

'Get out of here!'

'I think you should leave, Mr South.'

Rose's voice had taken a more positive edge now. Ben nodded, without taking his

eyes from Starling's. With a studied contempt he said, 'You dropped your cigar,
Mister Starling,' ground his foot into the
smouldering carpet and turned his back on
the head of Starling Enterprises. Rose came
out behind him, closing the door quietly.
Ben was headed for the corridor when Rose
called out to him.

'Mr South, I did try to warn you.'

'Yes.'

'I think it would be as well to heed Mr
Starling's warning, even if you were inclined
to ignore mine. He's a powerful man.'

'I'm aware of that.'

'Think carefully about it.'

There was no mistaking the edge in Rose's
tone. The steely eyes were locked with Ben's
and it was quite apparent that Rose was no
time-server; Grant Starling's interests were
Edward Rose's interests, and he would have
no compunction in executing Starling's
orders, whatever they might be.

'I already have thought about it,' Ben said
coldly. 'Like I told that old man, I don't
scare easily.'

'Mr Starling might not be young, but he
doesn't lack teeth. All I say to you, Mr South,
is that you should not be hasty in your judg-
ments. Think carefully before you do anything more in this matter, think carefully.'

'You're repeating yourself, Rose, so I'll do
the same. I don't scare easily!'

Everybody was giving Ben South sensible counsel. Rider had told him to drop further enquiries because he wasn't in with a chance of success. Pete Henley had as good as said that Ben was neglecting the business in his obsession with the mystery surrounding the circumstances of Joanna's death. And Rose was backing it all up by emphasizing that to a man of Starling's power Ben was more than merely vulnerable.

'He thinks I'd be a pushover!' Ben snarled to himself in the quiet of his own flat.

But that just about summed up the situation. If Ben tried to malign Philip Starling, if he tried to probe further into the relationship that existed between the dead man and the dead woman, Grant Starling would certainly have the money to make things difficult for Ben.

And for Pete too.

But would Grant Starling act that way, or was it all a matter of bluff, the moving of chessmen in a game of personalities? Ben couldn't be sure: Rose had certainly left the ultimate sanction unexpressed verbally but the threat had lain there in his hard eyes and he was Starling's man.

Yet Ben couldn't leave it alone. He

couldn't, he'd come this far and the questions still lay unanswered. He'd pressed the issues and he'd been met by evasion, and now at last by the threats of Grant Starling. If anything, it had the effect of only making him more determined.

The problem was now to determine what the next step should be. He worked at the office for the next few days and spent one afternoon with Pete Henley poring over plans for the first of the new hotels in the Cornelius chain but he was preoccupied and unable to concentrate on the work in hand. Once or twice he caught Pete looking at him with mingled anxiety and frustration in his eyes but nothing was said, and Ben knew that Pete was still licking his wounds after the last occasion when he had offered advice. He made no attempt to ask Ben about his interview with Grant Starling and Ben offered no information.

At the end of the week Ben had found no solution to his own problems but he had emerged from them sufficiently to realize that Pete too was worried – about something more than just Ben's preoccupation with Starling. It shamed Ben somewhat that he hadn't noticed earlier; he knew Pete well, and Pete carried his troubles in his face. When he was worried, it showed.

And he was worried.

He tried to pass it off when Ben finally

asked him about it, but once pressed he came out with it quickly enough.

'It's this Cornelius thing, Ben.'

'What's the trouble there? The contracts are signed, Emsley and the others will be joining the board at the end of the month, the capital injection should occur shortly afterwards and we move into the Cornelius Hotels project with all our guns firing. So what's the problem?'

'I don't know. I got a feeling.'

'Intuition, Pete? It's for the birds!'

'I was supposed to see Emsley yesterday to get his signature on the share certificate transfers. He didn't show.'

'He's a busy man.'

'He left no message, no reason for not showing either, Ben.'

'Well–'

'The day before that I tried to ring Cornelius and was put through to his secretary. All I wanted was to ask what had happened to the project plans for the first hotel that I'd put through to Cornelius's board of directors and Cornelius wasn't available.'

'I'd have thought he wouldn't need to be bothered about that sort of detail, Pete, it could have been dealt with by–'

'You don't get the point, Ben. That secretary's voice – she didn't want to know me.'

'Pete–'

'I'm telling you. She wanted no chat with

Henley and South Ltd.'

'I'm sure you're exaggerating, Pete.'

But next morning he discovered it was no exaggeration. Pete came into his room and flung on to Ben's desk a sheaf of papers. They comprised copies of recent contracts entered into by Henley and South Ltd and progress reports on the work in hand. When Ben looked up to Pete with a puzzled expression he saw that his partner's heavy face sagged with a frustrated disappointment.

'The way these papers show it, Ben, we've enough work to last us another month.'

'I know. That's the way we wanted it.'

'After that we're out of business.'

'What do you mean, Pete? The Cornelius contract will be giving us as much as we can handle so–'

'That's the crunch, friend.' Pete sat down slowly and shook his head. 'We did as Cornelius asked and took on no new work. We're scheduled to run till the end of the month – after that we'd be unable to whip up enough business to keep going, now – without the Cornelius Chain. And that, old friend, is no longer ours.'

He glared at Ben with angry eyes.

'Cornelius is pulling out.'

'But Cornelius can't back out of our deal! Hell, we've got a verbal agreement backed by a written contract. He can't just–'

'He can, and he is. Here's the letter that

arrived this morning, before you came in.'

Henley handed Ben the letter and Ben read it quickly.

'Dear Henley,

I thought it only fair to let you have due warning that I have this morning contacted the company solicitors with a view to bringing to an end the agreement between us concerning the Cornelius Hotel Projects. After due reflection I have decided that it would be in the interests of neither group to proceed; I may add that I now have some doubt as to whether the company you propose would be capable of handling the work involved, at the costing you made.

I have informed Sir John Emsley of the situation and it may well be that he would now wish to have no further association with your company, and consequently he may no longer wish to serve on your reconstituted board. These are matters you will have to take up with him, and the other people who agreed to become directors on your newly-formed board.

Yours sincerely,
P.R. Cornelius.'

Ben felt cold and sick. He placed the letter on the table and stared at it, then shook his head violently and pushed it back to Pete in disgust and anger.

'We can't let him get away with this, Pete. We've deliberately cut back on our contracts, we've not entered new agreements, we've negotiated for the hiring of machinery and equipment – hell, we'll lose a packet!'

'The new board won't get formed now, that's for sure. I tried to get Emsley on the phone but he's not available. Like Cornelius he's gone to ground – I tried for an hour to get hold of that feller. In the end I was put through to the company solicitor – I've fixed an appointment with him tomorrow.'

'Well we'd better get everything straight,' Ben said grimly. 'If we show Cornelius what we stand to lose and what we'd be claiming in a suit for breach of contract maybe we'll push them into carrying out the agreement.'

Pete Henley scowled.

'I reckon they'll have looked into that already – and won't be scared by it.'

Ben shook his head in puzzlement.

'But why? Everything seemed set fair – why should Cornelius back out now? He seemed to have faith in us, and it was he who wanted us to form a company in the first instance. What's made him change his mind?'

'Maybe we'll find out tomorrow, but in the meanwhile I suggest you put aside your problems with Grant Starling and get down to something more urgent. My office?'

'In five minutes,' Ben agreed. There was no choice about the issues; Starling and the problem of getting at him would have to wait. The future of Pete Henley and Ben South depended on it.

When they arrived at the office of the company solicitor next afternoon it was with a background of eight hours' solid work behind them. They had hammered away at what the loss of the Cornelius contract was likely to cost them and they had prepared watertight figures. They had made out an impressive financial case to persuade Cornelius that he should not withdraw from the completed agreement and as the final figures had emerged, late the previous evening, Pete Henley had become more cheerful. He'd suggested that Cornelius would be mad to pay out so much money for the pleasure of breaking a contract, and if he did still back out, at least the financial picture wouldn't be too black. They'd get adequate compensation under the breach clause in their agreement.

But Ben was unhappy. Something was niggling at him like an aching tooth and he couldn't decide what it was. The company solicitor kept them waiting for ten minutes and Pete prowled the room like a caged tiger but Ben sat still, thinking. He was concentrating on Cornelius the man, on his early reception of Ben South, on his interest in the building of a new company for South and Henley, and this turn-about now puzzled Ben. He picked up a prospectus for P.R Cornelius and Associated Ltd and stared at it but he did not see the words; anger and doubt clouded his mind.

At last the two partners were shown into the presence of Mr Daly, chief solicitor to P.R Cornelius. Daly was a dapper little man with a face as smooth and as expressionless as an egg, and he waved them to the chairs set precisely in front of his desk.

'Now then gentlemen, the ... ah ... the hotels agreement... Cornelius and ... ah ... Henley and South. You have been apprised of my Company's wishes in the matter?'

Pete fished in his briefcase and with a sour smile tossed the relevant papers across the desk to Daly. He was wasting no time.

'These figures should show you how unwise it would be for Mr Cornelius to back out of the contract now.'

'Figures?' Daly said, handling the paper with delicately arched fingers and twisting his lip slightly.

'Those figures will show you what it will cost Cornelius, if he breaks our contract.'

'Ah, yes, the contract...'

There was a doubtful air about the remark and Ben was angry.

'That contract is legally sound. It was agreed upon, signed by all parties. Cornelius handed us the hotels construction deal. He can't back out now.'

'He has every intention of doing so, I'm afraid.'

'Then it'll cost him!'

'Well, yes,' Daly said with a vacant smile, 'I suppose it will, to some extent, but he's prepared to take the loss.'

'At those figures?'

Pete's voice betrayed his astonishment but the look in Daly's sneering eyes made Ben feel that they hadn't yet heard the worst.

'Mr South, you agreed these figures with Mr Henley?'

'Of course.'

'Hmmm. They're far too inflated, you know. Mr Cornelius will not be paying you one half of that sum.'

Ben stiffened, glanced at Pete's suffused features and gestured him to silence. Quietly, he said,

'Those are carefully costed figures. We've done all that Cornelius asked. We've held off on contracts. We've taken no new work. We've hired equipment and machinery to the tune of several thousand pounds, and we've arranged for various hiring–'

'Have you read your contract, Mr South?'

'Of course I've read the blasted contract! What do you think we've been–'

'And Clause 15, sub-section 2?'

Ben hesitated.

The compensation clause,' he said.

'In our circles we tend to call it the break

clause,' Daly replied in a smooth tone. 'It's a standard clause we incorporate in all our agreements, quite straightforward, quite simple. It states, if you'll permit me to refresh your memory, that in the event of a breach by either party there shall be paid by way of agreed compensation a sum of money that shall cover all losses that arise naturally as a result of that breach.'

'I remember it.'

'That is why this "costed" sum you mention is totally unacceptable.'

Again Ben waved Pete to silence when his partner seemed about to burst out vehemently. In a cold anger Ben said,

'We're of the opinion that the clause covers us to the extent of the figures.'

'I hardly think so. I have glanced but briefly at your figures but already I can say categorically that no court of law would uphold them. Mr Cornelius would never be held responsible, for instance, for the vast sum you claim under the hiring agreements you'd be forced to break, or the loan charges incurred in raising finance for equipment and materials.'

'But they arise because he's breaking the contract!'

'Not so. They arise, not naturally as a result of the breach, but naturally as a result of your own impecuniosity. If you hadn't been short of money you'd have *owned* that equipment already, not been forced to hire it. It was your shortage of financial backing that made you hire, and the break clause will not compensate you. There is a clear decision on the matter,' Daly added and his eyes grew dreamy for a moment, 'reported in 1933: *Liesbosch Dredger v Edison*. I can summarize it for you, if you wish.'

'We couldn't buy such equipment, we *had* to hire it, we're a small firm.'

'That is your problem, Mr Henley. You can't expect Mr Cornelius to subsidize you into a better financial status.'

'But he's breaking an agreed contract!'

'And will compensate you. Under the agreement. Roughly ... at about one sixth of the claim you make.'

Ben almost had to restrain Pete Henley from grabbing at Daly. The solicitor paled, but was quite determined in spite of the angry flush on Henley's face.

'That's if you settle out of court,' he said firmly. 'If you sue we'll question every penny and there's some doubt as to whether you could afford that, in the long run.'

Ben had heard enough. He stood up, towering over the desk and the little man behind it.

'I want to see Cornelius.'

'That's out of the question. I'm empowered to–'

'I want to see Cornelius, not you. I want to

know why he's pulling out of a deal he was all set on a little while back. I want to see him and I mean to see him.'

'It's impossible.' Daly's little eyes glinted with malicious satisfaction. 'Mr Cornelius is abroad.'

'He wrote a letter to us the day before yesterday.'

'Mr Cornelius took the three o'clock flight out of London Airport yesterday afternoon. Now then, gentlemen, I suggest you go away and think about what I said. Consult your own solicitors; I'm sure they would paint a picture as clear as I, and not significantly different.'

Pete growled a short obscenity and stumped out of the room. As Ben glanced back, leaving the room, he saw a faint supercilious smile on Daly's face.

'Let's get a drink; I need one,' Pete said angrily as they made their way out of the building. Ben followed him into the taxi called for them and they went along to the unpretentious club that was frequented by businessmen like Pete Henley. Ben was no clubman himself.

He felt depressed and his puzzlement had increased, if anything. He could not understand what had happened to cause Cornelius to change his mind. As Pete gave his order to the waiter Ben stared at the pamphlet in his hand, the company prospectus he had brought from Cornelius's offices. He began to crumple it viciously, angrily; the paper twisted, and he caught sight of a list of the subsidiary companies run by Cornelius.

Pete turned around to speak to Ben but stopped when he caught sight of the fury registering in Ben's face; fury and despair.

'Where's the telephone?' Ben asked and Pete told him. Next moment, without another word Ben leapt to his feet and strode across the room, leaving the drink untouched upon the table.

CHAPTER 7

1

A cold bitter wind arose that evening, hinting at snow, but the warm fire in Pete Henley's sitting-room dispelled all thought of that from Ben's mind and the whisky that Pete had thrust into his hand glowed golden in the glass, warm and comforting.

'It's a long time since you've been around to see us, Ben,' Harriet said quietly.

Ben smiled at her. She was a small, slight woman with greying hair and a network of lines around her eyes but there was always about her an air of peace and compassion that made being near her a gentle, easing experience.

'I've stayed away too long, Harriet, particularly in view of your cooking.'

It was in a sense typical both of Harriet and Pete that when Ben had arrived this evening they had made him join them in their evening meal with no talk of business or other anxieties. He had come to spend an evening with them, and their friendship must come first. The meal had been a good one, as Harriet's always were, and their talk had been easy, as it had always been in this house.

But now, as they sat with their drinks before the open fire she knew it was time they talked about the problems that Henley and South faced.

'I understand from Pete that you saw Mr Cornelius's solicitor this afternoon.'

'That's right. I guess Pete will have told you what transpired too.'

Pete shifted heavily in the deep armchair and crossed one slippered foot over the other.

'I gave Harriet the general story. I told her that this broken contract is likely to ruin us.'

'We've faced trouble before,' Harriet said gently and when she looked at her husband Ben saw something in her glance that emphasized just how close this marriage was in human terms.

'Not as bad as this,' Pete said gruffly. 'I went to see our solicitors later, Ben, and they more or less confirm what Daly said. They feel he's painted a gloomy picture of course, but they don't think we'll win much out of the affair.'

'And it's all my fault,' Ben said.

There was a short silence. Pete cleared his throat noisily and a moment later Harriet murmured something about doing some work in the kitchen but Ben forestalled her.

'Don't go, Harriet. You've as much right to hear this as Pete. I've brought it on both of you.'

'I don't understand,' Pete said.

'Simple enough. Money talks.'

Harriet glanced at Pete uncertainly and Ben went on in a bitter voice.

'After we left Daly, Pete and I went for a drink and I was casually looking at the Cornelius holdings list in his prospectus. Now when we demanded to see Cornelius we were told he'd left the country. When I glanced at the prospectus I saw that one of his subsidiaries is a Canadian firm.'

Pete frowned; he seemed about to say something but subsided.

'You know just how much Canada has been on my mind of late. All right, so this firm's existence was coincidental. But I don't like coincidences and it gave rise to nasty possibilities in my mind. When the thought hit me I left Pete at once and made a phone call. I got London Airport to confirm for me that P.R Cornelius had left on the three o'clock flight yesterday afternoon. His destination was Vancouver.'

'You've already said Cornelius has at least one company in Canada.'

'They were also able to tell me that Grant Starling and his entourage took the same flight.'

Pete put his head back against the chair and stared at Ben through heavy-lidded eyes. His brow was ridged with doubt.

'You're not suggesting—'

'Don't tell me I'm seeing shadows without substance, Pete. Don't tell me again that I'm obsessed. It all fits, can't you see it? I went to Canada, I discovered a connection between Joanna and Grant Starling's son and I faced the old man with it. What happened? He bawled me out; he threatened me; he told me he could smash me.'

'All right, I accept that but—'

'There's no but about it. I told Starling and I told his man Rose that they couldn't frighten me off. I made the point strongly – they couldn't have failed to get the message. Now, a few days later, out of the blue, Cornelius breaks the most important contract Pete and I have had, for no apparent reason, and is quite prepared to pay compensation within the contract for the pleasure of doing so. Next day he leaves for Canada on the same plane as Grant Starling.'

186

'It sounds fishy but I think you're still jumping to conclusions.'

'It's all logical, Pete. Starling owns the biggest construction company in Canada. He didn't get there by being nice to people. I'll tell you what's happened to us. As soon as I left Starling's office he decided he wanted me settled; he wanted me fixed so I wouldn't push enquiries any further. It would be easy enough for a man with his backing to discover what I – and you – were up to in the business world. As soon as he learned we were tied to Cornelius he went straight to him. He told Cornelius to break my contract, pay limited compensation. And break me.'

'But why should Cornelius comply?'

'Grant Starling has already bought men to save his son's name. What's one more? He's bought Cornelius the same way he'll have bought others – with a promise of the big deal, under the Starling organisational set-up. That's why Cornelius will have gone to Vancouver. With Grant Starling.'

Pete shook his head doubtfully.

'It would have to be big, to make up for the compensation Cornelius will have to pay us.'

'That may be so; on the other hand there's the possibility that Starling's agreed to indemnify Cornelius for the compensation payable – for the pleasure of seeing my face rubbed in the mud and the satisfaction of having me off his back.'

All three sat silently for a while, Ben glaring into the fire, Pete lost in thought. At last, in a quiet voice, Harriet said,

'Is that what you're going to do now, Ben?'

'Leave Starling alone?' Ben shrugged disconsolately. 'What else can I do? I've brought all this on you and Pete as well as myself. I can't endanger your lives further; I must try to make up to you what you've lost through my pig-headedness. For Pete was right, as Rider was, when he told me I ought to back down. And that's what I'm going to do, right now.'

'Somehow that doesn't sound like you, Ben.'

'That's where you're wrong, Harriet. It's *just* me. I ran once before, from Canada, and I'm turning tail again right now. I caved in when Joanna died, and I'm caving in now. If I could reach Starling or his son ... but I can't. My fight now must be to save the business for you and for Pete and for myself. I've finished chasing shadows.'

A slow anger was seeping into Pete Henley's face marking his mouth with a viciousness at odds with his character.

'It doesn't seem right that a man like Starling can get away with this ... if what you say is right, Ben.'

'It is right and he can get away with it because he knows that with our business in jeopardy I'm going to have neither time nor inclination to bother him further.'

'Even so, I think–'

'No, Pete, there's nothing to discuss in the matter. What we have to do now is to straighten out the Cornelius affair as well as we can, come out of it with as few bruises as we can manage, get the business back on its feet and avoid the bankruptcy courts. The compensation we get won't even cover the hiring charges we've incurred so we've got to find ways and means to get enough work in hand to allow us to go to the banks and get them to advance us enough working capital to carry on during the next twelve months. It's going to be a tough, long haul.'

They spent the next ten days doing just that, taking out a writ against P.R Cornelius Ltd for breach of contract, instigating discussions between both firms of solicitors, negotiating with the equipment firms for breach of the hiring agreements, and frantically seeking new opportunities for contracts, finance and equipment.

And then, quite suddenly, it was all changed again and the urgent tenor of the time took a new meaning for him.

He had dined with Pete and Harriet and he returned to his flat at eleven. As he inserted his key in the lock he heard his telephone ringing. He hurried in and took it from the receiver to be told it was a person-to-person, transatlantic. It was Rider, in Vancouver.

'I've been in Montreal and just got back today to my office. There was a message for me on my answering device. Someone has been trying to contact me. I rang him just an hour ago, before calling you.' Rider paused as the line crackled. 'It was Billy Pearl.'

2

The garage at Waterton Park looked just as depressed as Ben remembered and from the fact that the road had not been cleared he could guess that Billy Pearl would have served even fewer cars than usual. January snows had come to the park and the mountain ranges were invisible against the grey sky, hidden by snow clouds. The drive up to the town had been hazardous with the car skidding violently on certain of the bends in spite of the fact that snow ploughs had cleared the road. The problem was that though the highway was relatively free of snow the wind was bitterly cold and black ice formed on the roadway, virtually invisible, treacherous in its glassy surfacing.

The road that led up to the garage had not been cleared as efficiently as the main highway below and the last slope up to the top of the rise proved too much for Ben's car. After several attempts to master the ice he finally gave up and swung the car into a side turning, locked it, and ploughed up over the slope, muffled to the ears and shod in snow boots. His breath whistled in his chest as he walked up, sending a white haze before him and he felt droplets of moisture freeze on the edge of his coat collar. Yet he was warm enough, toiling up the slope, for the exercise was stimulating and the wind failed to cut through the thick outer clothing he wore.

The snow was piled deep, drifting around the pumps, and it was quite obvious that Billy Pearl had not bothered, during the last few days, to go to the trouble of clearing a path. There would be precious few cars moving along here. Ben guessed that Billy's father would probably have seen this garage as a summer proposition anyway, dealing with the visitors to the International Park. During the winter months little would be moving.

Ben clumped his way across the snow towards the house. Billy Pearl opened the door to greet him and lend him a hand up the steps. He ushered Ben through into the living-room where a huge log fire roared.

'Here y'are, Mr South, thaw out here.'

'I'd almost forgotten how cold it can get up in the Rockies.' Billy Pearl nodded sagely. 'Better get out of them boots too,' he said.

He bustled through to the kitchen, a round, eager little man and came back with a pot of steaming coffee which he set down in the hearth. He poured a mug of coffee for Ben and one for himself and Ben smiled his thanks.

'Things are pretty quiet, Billy.'

'Always are, this time of year. The park gates stay open, but them shops below close up tighter'n ticks on a sheep's back. Ya know the population of the park in summer is around 10,000 but in winter it barely tops two hundred and fifty.'

'I can believe it.'

'I think that's maybe why the old man came out here,' Billy said sadly. 'Sure he wanted to run his own business, but he reckoned to make his pile in the summer, and come winter hole up in peace and content. It never worked that way; maybe like the old lady said, it was a judgment from above, the old man startin' out with dirty money...'

He turned his head to stare out of the window.

'Still snowin'.'

'Not much.'

'It snowed real bad our first winter here. There was fox, an' deer, an' lynx, coyote ... they all come down to escape the snow in the high country, ya know.'

Ben realized that Billy Pearl was trying to get at ease, trying to build a bridge between them, one he could cross to talk about what was really on his mind, the reason why he had phoned, the reason why Ben was here now.

'See any grizzly?' Ben asked softly.

'Thousand pounds of muscle, an' three inch spikes for claws. Yeah, Pop Bernard shot himself one last fall. You oughta meet Pop Bernard. He knows bear. He reckons them grizzlies is more honest than us, an' enjoy life better too.'

His chuckle died away. He sipped at his coffee, made a face and then looked up to Ben with sad brown eyes.

'But you don't wanna know about bears.'

Ben made no reply. After a moment Billy rose from the kneeling position he had adopted in front of the log fire and went out into the other room. He returned with a small notebook of cheap manufacture in his hand. He took up his position again and stared at the book, weighing it reluctantly in his hands.

'Goes to show how you c'n jus' never tell,' he said. 'You c'n be brung up by a feller, an' think you know him inside out and yet he's allus got his secrets from you, you can never get inside his skin. Take my old man, for instance. Honest Joe Pearl. He had an image, you know, back in Fairmont. An' I suppose he jus' looked at hisself one day and said sure, I got an image, but where's it got me? Nowhere. Or maybe someone said it to him.'

He slapped the book against his wrist,

smartly, in an angry gesture.

'When you called here before, Mr South, I told you not to put too much store by the old lady's letter – she was a real old-time Mormon and her soul was in torment. But after you'd gone, and after she passed on, and that feller came around working for you – the one I phoned–'

'Rider.'

'Well, after all that, trade fell away badly and the snows come in an' I was holed up here an' I got to thinkin' that maybe I ought to look through that junk out in the shed. I started to look but I left an oil lamp out there, it tipped over and the whole place went up in flames. And that, I thought, was that. But it wasn't – because last week I found this book.'

He held it up reluctantly.

'It wasn't out there in the shed at all. I should've realized that the old man wouldn't put out there any things he held real important. I found it in an oilskin that he allus kept wrapped under his bed. There was an old Colt in there, a watch-chain that belonged to his grandfather, a medal he won at a turkey shoot when he was sixteen, whole lot of things like that, you know, things that are important because they point to days in his life that he'd wanna remember. This … this book was there, because it would include a day he'd wanna forget. It's kinda…'

He struggled painfully for the word. Ben supplied it for him.

'Ironic.'

'Yeah.' Billy Pearl sighed and handed the book over to Ben. The surveyor took it gently, but made no attempt to open it.

'We don't know for sure, Billy, not for sure.'

'Stands to reason though, don't it? The old man didn't win the money to buy this place on no horse race. That was just a yarn he spun the old lady. Kept her quiet. But all the time he lived here it was eatin' away at him. Until he had to tell her, an' she had to tell you. Oh, I reckon we can be pretty sure, Mr South. Like you said, there was really only one connection between the old man and your wife and it was that inquest.'

He stared at the fire, his shoulders hunched.

'Jus' shows how you never get to know a feller, not even your old man. He had pride, you know, Joe Pearl had pride in hisself. Yet he perjured hisself. For money.'

'Billy–'

'No. It's in there, Mr South, it's all in there. He was a funny guy, Joe Pearl, he kept a record of all his financial transactions an' he put 'em down there, they go back years. When I found that book I kept it two days before I'd look at it. Then I looked. For the entry about them horses. There wasn't such an entry. But when I saw the entry he'd put down on that page – see, I turned the corner of it down – I knew I had to get in touch with you again. It'd be what you want. It … it was certainly somethin' *I* didn't want to see, that's for sure…'

But when Ben looked at it, the entry wasn't quite what he had expected to see, either.

Ben spent a day and a half kicking his heels in Red Deer, waiting for Rider to join him. On two occasions he almost went out to visit the Davises but each time he resisted the temptation to face them out. He and Rider had theorized enough; the proofs were now coming to hand and only when they had all the cards they could hope to get should they call their opponents. So he stayed in the hotel and waited.

He put in two calls to Pete Henley during that time to check whether Pete had had any success in raising the finance for a building project that they had decided to tender for while waiting for the outcome of the Cornelius settlement – for they'd decided to settle out of court rather than line lawyers' pockets. Pete reported that the finance hadn't been forthcoming and the tender had lost out against competitors. Henley and South were still deep in the wood. It left Ben frustrated, angry and guilty. But still, when Pete had heard that Rider had called him to say that Billy Pearl had found proof of a link between Philip Starling and Joe Pearl he had insisted that Ben go back to Canada and take it up.

'I can do all the worrying that's necessary back here,' he'd said gruffly. 'Leave it to me – you get out to Canada and break Starling's back for me. I want to see him brought to book now as much as you do.'

But Ben still felt guilty about leaving Pete with the business anxieties. Nevertheless, here he was in Red Deer, waiting for Rider. They had arranged that the enquiry agent should go to Shelby, Montana, to beard Sam Durrance, tell him the gates were opening and it would be as well if the ex-policeman told all he knew. While he was doing that Ben went straight to Billy Pearl at Waterton Park to collect the all-important proof that Billy had mentioned.

But Rider hadn't kept to schedule. Ben waited but the agent made no appearance until late in the afternoon of the second day.

Ben was glad to see him. They shook hands, and Rider slid gratefully into a chair to sit silently for a while staring at the ceiling. Ben observed him quietly; he was a small man, slim-shouldered, no more than five feet eight in height, but even when relaxed in a chair he gave an impression of athletic tightness; wiry muscle and sinew drawn into a coiled power spring. His jacket was open in the warmth of the hotel room and Ben saw the way his shirt stretched tight across his hard-muscled chest and flat stomach. His hair was cropped short, his eyes were a washed-out brown, his lips were thin and he rarely smiled, apart from the slight lifting at the corner of his mouth when he was amused. He had an air of seriousness, of committal to his profession. And he exuded an air of positive confidence that made Ben glad to see him.

'I'd expected you earlier.'

The brown eyes looked at him calmly.

'The train was late, after the flight took off behind schedule, after my cab got bogged down. It gets bad in winter.'

'I've heard. How was Shelby?'

'Cold.'

'And Durrance?'

'Colder.'

'How do you mean?'

Rider chewed thoughtfully on his lower lip.

'I called at his place in Shelby and it was up for sale. I guessed that maybe Sam Durrance had been thrown inside for another thirty-day stretch or so, and that he was selling up to raise some cash. I went around to the jail, and they soon disillusioned me.'

'Where was Durrance?'

'It's like this. He was released some five days after I saw him, you know, when he was

198

serving time for hammering the Court woman. Well, it seems he took up with her again when he got out. After I left the police I went along to see her and got some of the story from her. It wasn't difficult. He left owing her forty dollars.'

'Where did he go?'

'He came out of jail, spent a week with Mandy Court and during that time he acted rather mysteriously, hinting with some excitement that he was sitting on a gold-mine – her words. The upshot was that after a few phone calls he borrowed forty dollars from her and told her he was heading off to meet someone up in Chinook. She waited a while but heard nothing from him and she got to thinking about the forty he owed her so she went to the police and complained, telling them he'd lit out after taking the money from her purse.'

'She hasn't seen him since?'

'She hasn't and she won't.'

'He's completely disappeared?'

Rider scratched his short cropped hair with a single exploratory finger.

'Not completely. I found him, sure enough. I went along to Chinook – which sent my timetable all to hell – and I made a few en-quiries. No dice until I tried the morgue.'

'The morgue!'

'Sam Durrance is dead. Hit and run, north of Chinook.'

He stared impassively at Ben as the news registered. Ben swore angrily and smacked his open hand against the chair arm.

'I thought things were swinging our way!'

'They didn't swing Durrance's way, that's for sure. He's colder than the snow.'

Ben looked up into the washed-out eyes of the enquiry agent. There was something in Rider's tone that suggested this might have been more than a mere hit and run accident.

'What have the police in Chinook been able to find out?'

'After I identified Durrance they pulled in a vagrant and charged him with lifting Sam's wallet. But they have nothing on the car that hit Sam Durrance, nothing on car or driver.'

'The wallet–'

'Contained about twenty dollars. The vagrant must've found Sam's body, lifted the wallet, made it to town, got picked up by the police and swore he was handing it in as lost property – or about to. He didn't mention the stiff outside town. The police made no connection between the hit and run case and the wallet already in their possession – which was why they didn't inform Shelby police about Sam's death. Once I identified him they pulled in the vagrant again and threw the book at him.'

'But that leaves us no further forward. Another coincidence–'

'Maybe. But Joe Pearl and his widow are one case, Durrance is different. We could have leaned on him, maybe got something out of him. In Shelby he was a bum, and broke. But he left Mandy Court with a new lease of hope – "sittin' on a goldmine". It's *too* coincidental that he should cash his checks soon after.'

He linked his slim fingers together, leaned forward and eyed Ben carefully.

'So my trip was largely a waste of time. How about yours?'

'I got what we wanted.'

'The link between Philip Starling and your wife?'

'Not in so many words. You'll remember that Billy Pearl's phone message just said he'd come across papers that might support our theory that Starling had paid Joe Pearl money for something – probably to perjure himself.'

'That's right. Well?'

'We were never very specific with Billy; and he found the entry that was all-important to us, but it gave me something of a surprise when I read it. It's here in this small book.'

He handed it across to Rider, opening it at the relevant page.

'As you'll see it's a bald enough statement. "Received, five thousand dollars, drawn F.N Bank, cheque signed–"'

Rider was staring at the entry, his mouth

pursed in surprise. Ben leaned back in his chair.

'Signed not by Philip, but by *Grant* Starling!'

3

The snow was piled car-high by the roadsides. Earlier in the winter it had quilted the mountainsides, tufted the evergreens, clumped the roofs with marshmallow topping. Now it lay thick and heavy and deep, erasing the architectural defects of the town, giving the main town centre a cosy old-fashioned look reminiscent of lap robes and sleigh-bells, as a bright sun sparkled on the white overnight fall and the mountains emerged spectrally from high cloud banks and misted pine forests. The thermometer said twenty below, but it was dry and pleasant in the sun.

The two men sat in the car and waited. A woman drove up, parked her car, then crunched her way on foot towards the brick and stucco institution across the snow-buried lawns. She glanced curiously towards their car but they made no move.

'He's late.'

'It's a privilege you can enjoy when you're self-employed. Pass the coffee.'

Rider passed the flask to Ben and watched

him pour a little coffee into a cup. The woman was entering the main door of the Parkland Nursing Home. She did not look back. Ben finished the cup of coffee and screwed the plastic top back on the flask before replacing it under the dashboard. He glanced at his watch.

'He can't be long now.'

As though to support his statement a long low Buick slid into the driveway below them and began to climb the hill, bright red, a violent splash of colour against the startling white of sun-sparkled snow. Rider glanced at Ben.

'Here we go.'

They opened the car doors and got out. The Buick whispered past them and headed for the nursing home and the two men walked at a regular pace across the crunching snow of the car park until they came to the steps beside the single car space reserved for the owner of the home. He was standing beside his car, locking the door.

'Dr Nebbia?'

Graham Nebbia turned, smiled, squinted up into the sunshine.

'Yes?'

Rider's voice was pleasant but his face was stiff.

'My right hand is placed in my pocket. In that hand there is a gun, an automatic pistol of small calibre but heavy enough to punch a hole in your chest. Now I want you to just stand precisely where you are for a moment, quietly, considering what might be the consequences if you do anything rash.'

The smile had faded from Nebbia's face. His glance flickered doubtfully from Rider to Ben and back again.

'What – what is this?'

'Quiet, Dr Nebbia. Stand quietly and consider. Don't act rashly. Stand, and think, and relax.'

'But what do you want? Is … is this a stick-up? You're crazy, I've got nothing–'

'We just want to talk to you for a while.'

'Talk? But this–'

'I said, relax.' Rider's tone had hardened now. The doctor's eyes flickered over his face uncertainly but he stayed where he was. Rider nodded. 'Now listen carefully. The three of us will now go into your office. You will tell the good lady who attends to your wants that you will be in conference for a little while and that you are on no account to be disturbed. Understand?'

'No, I don't–'

'But you will. When we've spoken to you. Let's go, Dr Nebbia, and remember, just relax, and behave naturally.'

Ben walked behind the other two as they entered the nursing home. Strangely enough, hysterical laughter bubbled in his chest; the result of tension, it was nevertheless sparked by what was basically a farcical situation. But Nebbia did exactly as he was told. He snapped a quick remark to Mrs Anderson, who was surprised and didn't even look at Ben as he walked past. He wondered whether she would recognize him; he doubted it. A little while later all three of them were in Nebbia's office and Rider was casually peeling off his topcoat, and smiling at Ben.

Nebbia gasped in anger.

'What the hell is going on? You said you had–'

'An automatic pistol? I'm sorry, Dr Nebbia, but I'm not licensed to carry a gun. But I thought that the suggestion that I was carrying one would save a lot of argument on the steps of Parkland.'

For a moment Nebbia stared wildly at them, uncomprehending, and then his expression hardened.

'You two had better leave now,' he said thickly and reached for the telephone on his desk. 'I don't know what game it is you're playing, but I don't like being made to look a fool. If you're not out of here in two minutes I shall instruct Mrs Anderson to call the police.'

Rider sat down and Ben gazed around, selected a chair in the corner, and did likewise. Nebbia glared at them.

'I have no alternative then?'

'Oh, but you do, and you'll take it, because a call to the police might prove embarrassing.'

'We'll see about that!'

Nebbia lifted the receiver and began to dial. 'I'll call them myself,' he said.

'Yes, all right. Give them our names, while you're at it. Rider ... and South.'

The finger quivered in the telephone dial and sharp eyes flickered from one man to the other. Nebbia licked his lips. He was looking sick.

'I want you two out of here.'

'But not with the assistance of the police, eh? It wouldn't do your professional career much good, would it, if we told them what we know?'

'You know nothing!'

'Don't bank on it!'

Nebbia replaced the receiver slowly.

'I've nothing to talk to you men about. Please leave.'

'A few moments ago you were commanding, now you're asking. The trouble with you, Nebbia, you're a coward. You're weak, you lack guts. I'm glad. It makes the job easier for me, and Mr South. Mind you, you've got reason to be scared, haven't you?'

'I have no idea what you're talking about. I think I'd better ask Mrs Anderson to–'

'No. Don't move from your desk, or I might have to get violent.' Rider fingered his broken nose and smiled broadly. 'I didn't get this playing Postman's Knock, you know.'

Nebbia sat down abruptly. His hands were steady and he seemed to be getting control of himself. Ben guessed that he was over his initial shock, and was coming to terms with the situation. He would want to bluff this out, deciding that silence and the pleading of ignorance would suffice.

'All right. I've no idea what this is all about but you two ... gentlemen seem to want to talk. Let's talk. Do you have a topic in mind?'

'The one that's occupying yours at the moment – ever since I mentioned my companion's name.'

Nebbia sneered.

'I'm afraid I didn't quite catch it.'

'South.' The surveyor leaned forward coldly. 'You made a perjured statement at the inquest on my wife seven years ago.'

'You can't – that's not true!'

'You remember it well, then?'

'Remember? I ... I don't know what you're talking about.'

Rider folded his arms and regarded Nebbia with a slow contempt. He shook his head sadly.

'You're a poor liar, Nebbia, but I'll refresh your memory for you. Seven years ago a woman died in Fairmont Valley. An inquest was held, to look into the cause of death.

You gave it as exposure. You committed perjury.'

'No. If I said it was exposure, that's the way it was. I have never committed perjury. I would swear that on my mother's grave.'

Nebbia was leaning forward, speaking urgently, and there was an inexplicable sincerity in his tone. It could have been the result of fear, good acting, but Ben found the ring of conviction in the impassioned statement. He glanced at Rider, puzzled, and saw that Rider had been put a little out of his stride by Nebbia's tone also.

'You insist that–'

'It's the truth. I have never committed perjury.'

Rider pressed the point but with every repetition Nebbia grew in confidence, and a flush of anger came to his cheek. With a sinking feeling in his stomach Ben recognized the emotion in Nebbia as one of indignation. But if he had not perjured himself, what about Durrance, and Pearl? Was all this still wild supposition?

'Then tell us just why you were paid!'

'I don't know what you're talking about.'

'You were paid a sum of money by someone, to perjure yourself at the South inquest–'

'That's not true!'

Rider glanced towards Ben, uncertainly. As he did so Ben realized that what Nebbia could be saying was true – so far as he went.

'All right,' he said quietly. 'You weren't paid to perjure yourself – but you were paid to keep quiet about something, weren't you?'

The distinction was subtle but it was one that Nebbia had obviously drawn and he licked his lips nervously, unable to meet Ben's fixed stare.

'I don't know what you're talking about.'

Silence fell and the three men sat there, Nebbia shifting uncomfortably in his chair. Twice he opened his mouth as though to speak, order them from his presence, but each time his courage failed him, and he waited. Theirs must be the next move. He was anxious, and frightened, but not frightened enough. Rider cleared his throat.

'Dr Nebbia. I think it's time you got it quite clear, the position you're in. You're a professional man. You have a great deal to lose. Your nursing home. Your status. Your reputation. Maybe, your life.'

Nebbia looked up quickly. A nerve twitched in his lean cheek.

'You – you're beginning to sound absurd.'

'I can fill out the details for you, my friend. Let me put it to you like this. Seven years ago a woman died. An inquest had to be held into the circumstances of her death. Now someone wasn't keen that too much should be said at that inquest. That someone possessed money and influence. He used both. I'll admit one thing to you, Dr Nebbia – we don't know just what happened the night Mrs South died. But we can have a pretty good guess because the three witnesses at the inquest were all bought off.'

'*Three* witnesses?'

'That's right. Didn't you know the other two got handouts as well? Interesting... The point was, my friend, that they did. Now first there was Joe Pearl: he gave evidence relating to the vehicle. He was paid to suppress something. What was it, Dr Nebbia? Maybe you don't know. All right. The second witness also got a hand-out – Durrance, the policeman in charge of the investigation. What was he staying quiet about. Now the third witness was you. What I want to know is, why were *you* paid, and who paid you?'

Nebbia was shaking his head.

'I didn't know ... I mean, I don't know what you are talking about. I insist–'

'Insist away, feller. But listen, too. Joe Pearl is dead. He can't talk, can't give any information about that inquest. That left Durrance and you. Now I saw Durrance some time back, and he wouldn't tell me the time of day, but he got very excited about something. A little later he told his girl he was sitting on a gold-mine. I think he went out to Chinook then, to do a little gold-digging. Trouble is, the mine was deeper than he thought.'

'What do you mean?'

'I mean Durrance is dead. Killed by a hit and run. But his death *is* a coincidence, isn't it?'

Nebbia's face was white.

'What are you trying to say?'

'I'm trying to say that there were two people who could have talked about that inquest. One of them had been paid off once, seven years ago, but I guess he thought he could wring a little more out of the man who paid him. I guess what he received was a car fender under his breastbone! And that leaves just one man, one witness, who knows about what happened to Joanna South!'

'You're crazy! These insinuations! I haven't tried to…'

'Tried to pick up any more cash? Does that matter too much? Durrance did, and is now safely out of the way. But you are still around, and you're the only positive threat now, aren't you? Tell me, have you been in touch with him recently? What did he have to say? Did he ask you to meet him in some dark alley? If he does, are you safe in going?'

'You're trying to frighten me!'

'No. I don't need to; you're scared enough because you've got reason to be scared. And you'll stay that way just as long as you're the only one who can provide evidence about that inquest! Once you tell us, you're clear, because the reason for removing you has gone. Your employer would be too late.'

'I … I need time to think!'

'Time to think means time for your employer to reach a decision! Don't be stupid, Nebbia! Durrance is already on a slab in Chinook! You want to join him?'

Nebbia was rubbing his hands together nervously, his eyes flickering glances from Rider to Ben and back again. He was frightened and he was confused.

'I need time, time to think this out! I don't understand – where you going?'

Rider was rising to his feet, motioning to Ben to do likewise. He shrugged.

'You're a fool, Nebbia. But then, maybe you've got nothing for us, anyway. We'll do it other ways. I just hope you're still around when we get to the man who paid you.'

Nebbia started forward, his face ashen.

'No! Wait. Just let me think a moment, let me get things straight! I didn't know about Durrance and Pearl! That wasn't what I was told, I understood it was just to prevent the family being distressed. I…'

His voice died away. He realized he had now said too much not to go on. He sat down helplessly as Rider stood in front of his desk glaring down at him.

'Let's have it all,' Rider said in a voice gritty with contempt. Nebbia shook his head slowly, helplessly, and looked out to the lawns of the Parkland Nursing Home.

'I can't,' he moaned. 'I can't tell you. It

was nothing, nothing that I did!'

'You suppressed information! You suppressed information that would show Mrs South did not die of exposure! She was murdered, wasn't she, Nebbia, murdered! And that makes you an accomplice after the fact!'

'No! No! That's not so!' Nebbia glared wildly at the two men facing him and then suddenly leaned back in his chair, both hands pressed against his jaws. He nodded. 'All right, I'll have to tell you. This man Durrance... I didn't know...'

He collected himself with an effort.

'But it wasn't the way you said. I had a practice in Fairmont, and I acted for the police from time to time. It was a small force. I had a call that day from the department to undertake a post mortem on a woman called South, who had been found dead in Fairmont Valley. I undertook the examination, and prepared my findings. Then I had a phone call...

'All right, I can't excuse what I did. But the caller was persuasive. He told me that to publish the findings would help no one and hurt too many people. He said he was acting for an interested person who didn't want to be involved, but there was also the matter of the woman's family to consider. He persuaded me finally that silence would be the best policy–'

'The persuasion,' Rider commented contemptuously, 'amounting to a nice fat fee!'

Nebbia nodded.

'Yes. I was paid for my silence. I went to the inquest, I gave my evidence and … and I collected my fee. Shortly afterwards I bought Parklands and–'

'And you've lived off the fat of the land ever since!'

'I did nothing wrong, as I saw it! I was simply being asked to withhold some irrelevant findings–'

'What the hell do you mean?' Ben felt anger rising in him. 'Did she or did she not die of exposure?'

'She died of exposure as I said at the inquest! There wasn't a mark on her, I swear! If there had been any doubt in my mind, any suspicion of foul play, do you think I wouldn't have voiced it? Do you think I would have withheld any evidence of that nature? I didn't know about the other two witnesses being suborned; it was a clear case of accidental death as far as I was concerned and the request I received seemed not an unreasonable one! I don't see how I acted badly!'

'Then why did you refuse to see me the first time? Why did you act like a scared rabbit as soon as you heard my name, and refuse to speak to me? Why did we have to indulge in this nonsense today, just to get to question you?'

'I … I…' Nebbia was at a loss to explain. He waved his hands ineffectually, and glanced wildly around him. 'I can't explain. It's just that the name, it was one that … that's been on my mind intermittently, all these years, and when I heard it I just panicked, and–'

'Because you knew that you acted unprofessionally, criminally even, seven years ago!'

'Unprofessional, yes, perhaps it was unprofessional, but there was no criminality involved. I was innocent of any design. I didn't know what was happening. I still don't! I don't know why you are pestering me, I don't know what you want from me!'

'We're pestering you because we want the truth!' Rider's face was grim. 'Your testimony at the inquest, was it accurate and true as far as it went?'

'Yes, yes! She died of exposure.'

'But you were paid to suppress some information?'

'Yes! But I–'

'Who paid you?'

Nebbia hesitated then plunged on. It was too late to resist.

'A man called Haggett. James P. Haggett.'

Rider turned a puzzled face to Ben. The name meant nothing to him.

'All right. The information you were to suppress?'

'Two post-mortem findings.' Nebbia shook

himself suddenly and sat more erect. He glared malevolently at Ben South. 'The first was evidence of sexual intercourse shortly before death!'

CHAPTER 8

1

Ben sat very still. He could see the vicious satisfaction in Nebbia's eyes, pleasure at being given the chance to strike back in some measure at his tormentors. He was waiting for Ben's reaction, hoping it would be a violent one. Ben knew it, understood the perverted pleasure it would give to Nebbia and he sat very still, and kept himself tightly under control. Disappointment crept into Nebbia's face and with it uncertainty. For a moment he had felt himself master of the situation, but now it was no longer so again. Rider did not look in Ben's direction. He said nothing, waiting for Ben's reaction. Ben put the next question in level tones.

'Are you saying my wife was raped before she died?'

There was still a flash of spirit in Nebbia as he realized the implications of the question.

'Oh no! I told you before – she didn't have

a mark on her body. I'm telling you there was evidence to show that during the hours before she died she'd had sexual intercourse, and it had been with her consent. You won't like hearing that, Mr South, but those were my findings!'

A lover. She'd been meeting a lover in Fairmont Valley, and they had been together and she'd left to drive to Mary Davis and she'd skidded and died there in the snow. Ben felt numb. A strange numbness, occasioned by the impression that he could never have known Joanna. He'd loved her, married her, lived with her – but he couldn't have known her. He would never have thought it possible that she–

'You said there were two findings suppressed.' His own voice startled him with its grating quality. 'What was the second?'

Nebbia hesitated.

'You must understand the way it was. When Haggett phoned, he said there'd been a bit of a party and the man, his client, didn't want to be involved, and it would only bring considerable distress to the woman's family, her husband, if–'

'What was the other finding?'

'She'd been smoking marijuana!'

Ben smashed his fist on Nebbia's desk.

'This is ridiculous! You're lying in your teeth! What you're telling me is impossible!'

'South–'

'No, Rider, this man's lying! He's trying to tell me my wife was a hophead, and was sleeping around as well! I *knew* her, Rider! Nebbia, if you don't come out with the truth I'll–'

Rider seized his arm; his fingers locked fiercely around Ben's wrist.

'Go easy, Mr South.' He turned to Nebbia. 'If you're lying–'

'You think I'm crazy? What's the point of lying now? All right, he thinks his precious wife was white as snow! Can I help it if he was a blind fool? I'm telling you the truth!'

He stuck to it for the next ten minutes, while Rider attempted to break his story and Ben sat angrily watching and listening. It seemed incomprehensible to him; he couldn't believe that he could be so wrong about Joanna. She had sounded odd and strained that last time he had phoned, they had been drifting apart certainly, but for Nebbia to suggest–

He cut in on Rider's questioning.

'Marijuana. Was there any evidence of addiction?'

'I couldn't tell that, not really. All I know is she'd been smoking before she died. That's it!'

And there they had to leave it.

They drove back on the Fairmont highway until they reached Valley Fork. Neither man spoke until the Fork, then Rider drew the car in against the piled snowbank and lit a cigarette. A car flashed past them, horn blaring and Rider made a rude, angry gesture. He turned to Ben.

'You're the boss.'

'The next step is obvious. I've got to see Seth Davis.'

'You think he'll tell you anything?'

'He could be the one.'

'My money's still on Philip Starling. Or...'

Ben glanced at Rider enquiringly. Rider shrugged and started the car. 'Just let me check, first.'

They drove on to the outskirts of Red Deer in silence. At the first drive-in they bought hamburgers and coffee, and Rider got out and went back to make a phone call. When he returned he was nodding to himself.

He settled himself in his seat and reached for his 'burger.

'You remember I said once it was no good chasing this thing further because Philip Starling was dead. Well, I was wrong, and I admit it. I just rang the number that Nebbia gave us, you know, this fellow Haggett's number. I asked the right dumb questions of the switchboard and got what I wanted. James P. Haggett is a lawyer. He works for a company. It's owned by none other than our old friend Grant Starling.'

'What are you driving at?'

'Just this. I was wrong to suggest you

backed down. You see, Joe Pearl was paid by a cheque signed by Grant Starling. Nebbia's payment came later, when Starling had had time to arrange things better. It was paid through Haggett. Now I've been assuming that Philip Starling ... knew your wife. But there's also the possibility that she was introduced to the old man!'

'You mean–'

'I mean there's no reason why we shouldn't go hell for leather after Grant Starling to get the truth of all this. Because whether it was he or his son who ... was with your wife, Grant Starling sure as hell paid the witness bills and sure as hell knows all about this thing. Even when Grant Starling was facing you, he was as guilty as they come!'

2

Mary Davis's pleasure and excitement at seeing Ben South was patent. She stood in the doorway and her face was flushed. She spread her arms wide, laughed aloud and grabbed for him, hugged him, dragged him forward.

'Ben! Why didn't you tell me you were back in Red Deer, and so soon too! Come in, for goodness' sake, and bring your friend with you! What on earth–'

Even as she pulled him in through the

doorway her smile began to fade. The implications of his sudden descent upon her home were still a mystery to her but then she saw who the 'friend' was and she recognized him; all three were quickly conscious of the tenseness of the atmosphere in the sitting-room.

'I'm sorry, Mary,' Ben said awkwardly. 'I couldn't give you warning sooner. It's ... er .. it's Seth I really want to see, and it's rather urgent.'

'Seth?' Mary still struggled with an excitement that was not yet dispelled. 'Seth's not here; he's gone down to Fairmont. You'll remember Frank Carson – the engineer? He was to get married when the dam was completed, well, he's changed his mind, though Seth reckons that nature has changed his mind for him, but anyway he's getting married tomorrow. Tonight he's holding his stag, and most of the men from the dam are going along. Seth had some business in town as well so he went off early to...'

Her voice died away as the anxiety grew in her eyes. She glanced at the silent Rider.

'What is it you want with Seth?'

Ben shuffled uncomfortably.

'I think we'll get on down to Fairmont and–'

'It's about Joanna again, isn't it?'

Her voice was dull and she turned away abruptly to stand with her hands on the

221

back of an easy-chair. 'Why can't you leave it alone, Ben?'

'It's gone too far for that, Mary. Much too far.'

'What is it you want from Seth? He can't help you – he knows nothing about what happened to Joanna!'

Ben hesitated, glancing at Rider as though for support. Rider shrugged, and moved towards the door. Mary turned at the sound, and her eyes were angry. 'What is it you want from Seth?' she demanded.

'Mary, that time Joanna was coming down here. You say she didn't phone?'

'No. She usually did, but not that time. She–'

'Had she ever met Philip Starling?'

'Who?' The question was instinctive, leaving her time for thought and manoeuvre. 'I … I can't remember.'

'Seth introduced them, didn't he?'

'Well, I … yes, I suppose he did, at least I think he did, but you don't suppose that Joanna would–' Her voice died away again. 'I didn't want to know, Ben, and I still don't. But leave Seth alone.'

'Was Joanna coming down to meet Starling?'

'I'm sure she wasn't!'

'But she didn't phone you.'

'Well, no, but–'

'But what?'

222

'I wasn't at home all day, I mean I came back late in the afternoon, and Seth had gone out and there was a chance that she did phone and got no answer–'

'You told me earlier that Seth was home working!'

'Well he was, in the morning, but she didn't phone to warn us and–'

'Mary. Let's have this straight. Isn't it true that she *could* have phoned, and Seth could have answered?'

Her face was racked with indecision and Ben suddenly realized that these were questions that she would have had at the back of her mind for years. Questions she would not have wanted to press upon Seth for he had told her what she had wanted to hear, and in his remarks had lain the safety of her marriage, the bulwarks against any crumbling of their relationship. Ben saw the pain in her eyes now and knew he could ask her no more.

'Never mind, Mary. I'll go see Seth. We'll let ourselves out.'

He had reached the door when she suddenly called his name, desperately. He turned, and she was staring at him with fear in every line of her body. Then, as he watched, he saw her harden, saw her determinedly bury her head again.

'It's nothing,' she said quietly. 'Nothing.'

The door closed quietly behind him.

It was early afternoon now and the sun had gone, to be replaced by heavy grey snow clouds. The wind had risen and it seemed even colder than before. The Rockies no longer scarred the skyline with their pinnacles of white; the sweeping clouds settled like grey blankets over the rocky heads and whispered down across the crags, into the valleys and over the hills.

'You think Seth knows more than he's said.'

Ben nodded, keeping his eyes on the icy road. Conditions were bad, as bad as he'd known in Alberta as far as temperature was concerned and if those snow clouds were as laden as they seemed to be the roads could well become impassable before next morning.

'Yes, I think he does. I'm just wondering how deeply he's involved in it all. I mean, Nebbia and Joe Pearl and Durrance, they all came in late, they were just keeping quiet at the inquest. We know now why Nebbia kept quiet and what he kept quiet about; I suspect Seth will be able to tell us what Durrance and Pearl could have said, but didn't. I'm beginning to think that he was with Joanna the night she died. That was no straight answer from Mary – it wasn't the story I got before. I suspect that Joanna phoned all right, and Seth took the call while Mary was out. Perhaps he went to meet her. The rest

… well, maybe Seth will be inclined to tell us. With a little persuasion,' he added grimly.

The light was fading quickly as they drove into Fairmont, even though it was only mid-afternoon. The snow clouds were low over the hills and it was bitterly cold. It reminded Ben of the days he had spent in the river valleys when the temperatures made metal objects burn to the touch and ungloved hands froze to tools and vehicles; earth and gravel shovelled into truck beds froze hard to the steel and wouldn't dump out. Now as they came over the hill into the town they caught a glimpse of twinkling lights across at the sulphur creek.

'Salamanders,' Ben explained. 'The workers over there have set up fire pots made out of punctured oil drums. It's one way of keeping warm.'

There was plenty of warmth in the long bar of the Royal Hotel. Rider parked the car while Ben went straight in. They had had to make only two enquiries in the town as to where Frank Carson's stag party was taking place, and when Ben arrived he was not surprised because the bar was packed to capacity and the party was already in full swing.

'Hell's bells,' Rider exclaimed in awe as he joined Ben just inside the door. 'Middle of the afternoon, too!'

His remark was overheard by a lurching drunk making his way towards the door by hanging on to the wall.

'Afternoon, nothin'! We been at it since breakfast!'

It was probably an exaggeration, but it was certainly true that the party had been swinging for some hours. Ben grimaced at Rider.

'We'd better split up. I'll move along to the left, you take the right. As soon as you find Seth, drag him back across to the door. We won't be able to talk in here; we'll have to get him out somewhere.'

Rider nodded and moved off. It was good sense. The babel of raucous voices made normal conversation impossible and there was a continual shoving and pushing of bodies as those standing at the bar made way, or were forced to give room to others fighting their way forward. There must have been over a hundred people in the long bar, and there was a continual flow of movement, across and through the bar, among the tables and through into the three small rooms leading off, open-doored, from the main room. To all Ben's enquiries he got the same reply: 'Seth Davis? Sure, he's here somewhere! Hey, ain't you gotta drink?'

Ben completed his tour of half the room and saw Rider coming towards him. His face was red and someone had spilled beer down the front of his coat. He shook his head.

'He's been here, but I'm damned if I can find him!'

'Did you see Frank Carson then?'

'I wouldn't know him if I saw him!'

'I'll look for him; he might be able to tell us what's happened to Davis.'

Ben pushed his way through the crowd and into the first of the anterooms. He tried bawling Carson's name but it had little effect upon the company. He met Rider just outside the door.

'Whoever pays for this little lot is going to have quite a bill to foot!'

'The hell with that! Where's Carson?'

'Someone lookin' for me?'

Ben whirled around to see Frank Carson standing there grinning at him, jostled by lurching men, slapping his back as they moved past. Ben grabbed for his arm.

'Frank – can we have a word?'

'As long as you have a drink as well!'

Surprisingly, Carson was still sober, or else he held his liquor well. Ben shook his head at the proffered bottle.

'This is important. Come out into the lobby with us.'

It was easier to say it than to do it for where Frank Carson moved an eddy began, spreading out into a swirling mass of men eager to drink his health, talk to him, urge him to song, assure him it was a ring-a-ding stag. They fought their way through to the lobby however and crossed towards the stairs. There were some chairs on the first landing and Ben headed for these. The noise level was much lower here, though there were occasional forays of construction men into the hallway below.

'Phew!' Rider gasped. 'They're certainly giving you a send-off!'

'All due to the boss – says I deserve the best, an' he's paying for it so who'm I to complain?'

'Where is Seth?'

'You want to see him, Mr South?'

'Urgently.'

Carson was quite sober. Ben knew it now as the engineer's eyes fixed on his.

'What's it about?' Carson asked quietly.

'Nothing I can discuss with you, Frank. I'm sorry, but that's the way it is.'

'I've been wonderin' whether I'd see you again.'

'Well, you have. But it's Seth I want to speak to. Can you tell me where–'

'It's about that day up at the spillway dam, isn't it?'

Ben felt Rider move up closer just behind his left shoulder. Stiffly, he said to Carson,

'What do you mean? What about that day?'

Carson looked unhappy, scratching at his cheek uncertainly.

'Well, I don't know. It was a nasty affair, that accident of yours. I wondered later whether you might not think that Seth had been a mite careless. In fact, I wondered

228

myself. That's why I checked the sheared pin, later, after you'd gone. Took a good look at it. I just thought you'd like to know that the pin, well, it just went, that's all. I don't think it could have been foreseen. It was a pure accident. On the other hand–'

'Well?'

'I don't know. You two, were you just joking or somethin'? If so, it's a damn' stupid thing to do. But if Seth did it, and you got stuck maybe he didn't like to confess to it later and–'

'You're not making yourself clear.'

'You was stuck down on the ledge.'

'So?'

'You was stuck because the power was shut off. I was starting to drive down, coming down alongside the lake when that power was shut off. The switch is located in the control house, and there's a link with the lights along the dam too. One of them lights was still burning, I noticed it, and I saw it go out as I was driving down. When that light went out, the power to your cage was shut off.'

He hesitated, sheepishly.

'Seth was up in the control house.'

'You mean he could have shut off the power?'

'Well, yes, I guess he was just playing a joke, and didn't like to admit it later. I mean, the power came back on, didn't it? And that pin shearing, that was an accident.'

Ben didn't look at Rider. In a flat voice he said,

'That'll be about the size of it. Forget it, Frank. Thing is, where's Seth now? I want to see him – not about the dam, though.'

'He was here, but he got a phone call, and left. Told me it was important, he was sorry he had to leave.'

'It wasn't Mary, was it?'

'No, not Mary. He's gone up to Fenokee. Someone up there must've rung through.'

'We'll get up after him.'

'I'd leave it, Mr South. Near forty-mile drive, you know, and looks like snow.'

'We'll make it.' Ben waved goodbye and turned on his heel, collected his coat from the cloakroom downstairs and went out to the car with Rider.

The enquiry agent said nothing until he had started the car.

'What about this dam incident?'

'Like Carson said, maybe Seth was joking.'

Ben's tone was harsh and Rider glanced at him.

'You don't sound convinced.'

'You're damn' right. I'm not convinced. Seth may have been in the control house when that switch was pulled to cut off the power, but from what he said at the time, when the power came back on he was on the dam wall. Seth may well have cut off the power, but he didn't put it back on again.

Which means he didn't want that cage to come back up!'

3

It was snowing heavily when they drove out of Fairmont and took the road west towards the Fenokee Dam. Darkness fell soon after they left the town behind them, but fortunately the snow ceased falling and it proved not too difficult to drive while they were on the main road. The white sparkle of the snow threw dancing gleams under their headlights as they swept along, their tyres hissing sibilantly through the thick whiteness of the road. Few cars seemed to have passed along the west road and soon the few tracks that were already ahead of them petered out as they swung off the main road to take the highway leading up to the foothills below Fenokee. Rider drove with care under Ben's direction, though Ben was not familiar with the route; the only occasion he had been to the dam was when they had driven from Red Deer on the back road that Seth had used. Nevertheless, it proved not too difficult because once they were into the foothills yellow markers pointed the way; Fenokee had proved to be a tourist attraction of late months and was well signposted.

Progress was fairly slow since Rider took

no chances on an icy and unfamiliar road. Within the hour a moon, full and bright, drifted from behind the snow clouds and illuminated a ghostly landscape about them; high silent drifts, white and spectacular in their shapes and height, tall trees, black-centred and snow-capped, and once the slow twisting mercury silver of the river, glistening down towards Fairmont. As they drove higher a cold mist rose under the ice-sheathed trees and the spectral masses of the mountain peaks lifted gleaming peaks in a jagged frieze outlined against a black and grey sky. Twice their headlights caught the gleam of eyes in the darkness, flashpoints of light, startling in their intensity and quick leaping away, and as they breasted one rise they saw above them the dark shapes of a bighorn ram and its herd, an eight-point buck and two other mule deer, silhouetted against the white snow under the hill.

The tyre noise had changed now that they were higher; the hissing of fresh snow had changed to a harder crunching sound that intimated to them that the snow they had experienced in Fairmont had passed the hills and they were meeting icier conditions. It was certainly bitter cold, and though the heater was boosting warm air into the car both men were aware of the frosty air out-side, misting the rear window and harshening the glare of the headlights. Neither man had made reference to the dam incident again, and apart from occasional remarks concerning the route each had kept his own counsel.

It was Rider who broke the silence.

'You said that Seth perhaps didn't want that cage to come back up. But you weren't in danger, were you?'

'I don't think so. The cofferdam was due to be destroyed but where I was situated on the ledge I think I was reasonably safe. I might have got my feet wet, but the chances of my being in danger were relatively slim. It was a different matter, of course, when I went up in the cage and then dropped – the force of my descent took me past the ledge and straight into the path of the waves from the blasting.'

'That chap Carson said the shearing of the pin was accidental.

'Ahuh. I'd still like to ask Seth about the whole thing. It wasn't a pleasant experience in any case, and it wasn't necessary, if Seth did throw that switch as Carson wonders.'

They drove on, bumping over rutted snow which had probably been carved about by heavier vehicles working at the dam site. At one point they hit a rut violently and Rider momentarily lost control; in struggling for a lower gear he stalled the car and when he attempted to drive off after restarting there was a screaming of wheelspin from the back. Ben got out and pulled a shovel from the back of the car, together with a length of wire mesh which he pushed under the back wheels to give them purchase. Hacking the snow into a less hard-packed and smooth state made him blow hard and his breath froze on his upturned collar until bristles of ice thrust out from his face like starched, shining needles. He was glad to get back to the warmth of the car when it finally lurched out of the rut.

Once more they were forced to stop but this time it was on the crest of a rise and the road forked. There was a signpost pointing the way but it glistened under a sheath of ice and Ben found it necessary to use the shovel to crack the covering before he could read its message. When he got back to the car and pointed the way Rider was peering through the windscreen.

'What the hell's that?'

The peaks of the Rockies soared blackly above them and to the west, white-tipped under the fitful moon, but it was the long white arms reaching down into its valleys that had caught Rider's attention. The black mass of the mountains seemed to be smothered in parts by a white octopus that sent long tentacles out to hang into the narrow cascading valleys.

'The Columbia Icefield,' Ben said shortly. 'I told you they were trying to reroute some of the ice movement; some of it will be coming down into the Fenokee flow.'

'Not in that state, it won't. Hell, how deep is it?'

The city detective was driving off and it was a rhetorical question but Ben had heard that the ice, which flowed like lava over the cliff edges, was a thousand feet thick on the skyline. On the icefield itself it would go as deep as three thousand feet; new snow pressing down each winter would make the bottom warmer, and more plastic, and the result would be an advancing tongue, breaking off into blocks as big as freight cars. Up among the hills above the spillway dams the engineers would have been gouging out new channels in that white landscape, working to improve the flow to Fenokee across a wind-scoured, crevasse-gashed area.

Rider was checking the mileage. The last signpost had stated seven miles to Fenokee, and they had covered four since then.

'Should be getting sight of it soon,' Ben said.

Five minutes later they saw it.

First they passed a chalet, weatherbeaten, dark, deserted, stark against the shining snow and then there was a long dirty-white tongue of ice under the lodgepines, lapping a small frozen lake. Beyond was the waste of a construction site, huge heaps of dark gravel and boulders, thrown aside almost like the moraine of a retreating glacier. It was a drab area, soil-less, but it opened out dramatically

235

to an arena cluttered with cars and then the broad sweep of the glistening dam, and the vast ice-littered lake of Fenokee.

'Holy cow!' Rider, the city man, murmured and drove into the car park.

The moon rode high above the clouds and the lake sparkled, throwing off a tremendous sheen and reflecting in glowing patterns the lights gleaming from the control centre of the dam and the hutments grouped around the edge of the man-made camping area. Though he had seen the dam before Ben was as impressed as Rider; Fenokee had grown in size and splendour and under the moon it seemed too spectacular to be real. A light mist shimmered at the far end of the lake, ghosting the darkness of the tree-lined shore into a distant grey and the two men sat there for a moment staring at the sheer beauty of the scene. Then Rider stirred and glanced at Ben, and the surveyor nodded, and opened the car door.

As he did so headlights sprang to life in a car parked over near the control centre. Rider got out of the car and was locking the door when the vehicle from the control centre drove carefully past the parking area, trundling slowly towards the steep slope of the road running north through the trees. It churned past them, picked up speed as it hit the slope and then its red rear lights glimmered through the trees until it was lost to view and there was only the fading thunder of the engine, throbbing deep in the harsh, cold silence.

Ben was staring after the vehicle thoughtfully. Rider waited, then asked him what was the matter. Ben shook his head.

'Something about that car. Seemed familiar, somehow.' He realized why it seemed familiar some ten minutes later at the control centre when the engineer nodded, and hitched at his jacket before speaking.

'Yup. That was Seth Davis's car. He's been up here an hour or more, waitin' for Mr Starling to come back. Then Davis took them all off in his car, like Mr Starling suggested.' He looked serious suddenly. 'This bloody cold. Seems there's trouble up there. So they went to look.'

'Trouble?'

'Right. Up at Davis's spillway dam.'

CHAPTER 9

1

Rider's driving had now become imbued with a greater sense of urgency. It was not that anything of great significance had occurred, although the prospect of seeing both Davis and Starling together was one that caused Ben's pulse to quicken with a vicious anticipation, but the fact that they seemed to be nearing the end of the trail brought an excitement into their veins which was translated into a greater speed over the hard rutted snow. Iridescent gleams flashed from the icy branches of the lodgepines and aspen as the headlights of the car flickered and danced past them, and in the glow from the dashboard Ben could see the tense set of Rider's jaw as he concentrated on keeping the car on the track. They were assisted out in the open by the bright moonlight, fitful though it was and darkened by drifting snow clouds, but under the trees the glow of the snow was their only aid as it reflected the white headlights with a ghostly ambience.

'What do you reckon is the trouble up there?'

Ben shook his head.

'Maybe something concerning the construction – this cold could bring about a contraction in the construction, or maybe they've been having trouble with frozen concrete, I don't know. You can keep the concrete in a reasonable state by preheating the mixture, and we used to keep retaining forms warm by spraying them with jets of steam, but maybe they've had a breakdown in equipment.'

'From what you said back home the spillway dam should be near completion, though.'

'I would have thought so – but if the weather's been this cold it could have slowed the whole schedule. Anyway, that's just one problem they've got; we'll be bringing them another.'

'And I don't think they'll be welcoming us,' Rider said in a grim tone.

He changed gear as the road suddenly dipped over a ridge and dropped into the darkness of the trees. He braked slightly and the rear wheels locked, glissading the car down over the icy track, slipping sideways, bumping against the hard packed snow at the side of the road. Rider managed to keep the car heading in roughly the right direction but it was fortunate that the track swung right at the bottom of the slope so that he was able to pick up speed into the bend and drive into the rise of the next incline. As the nose of the car lifted into the hill its headlights briefly swung and flashed over copper wires sheathed in ice, gleaming under the trees like silver lines, sagging and stiff. They were power lines and telephone wires and Ben remembered seeing them on his last visit to the spillway dam; he knew now there was not much farther to go.

Even as the thought crossed his mind Rider began to roar. He braked, swung at the wheel, hesitated, and then suddenly with a quick change of mind slapped his foot hard on the accelerator. Paying less attention to the road ahead Ben had not seen what was happening, but Rider's manoeuvres caused him to look ahead and he saw what had occasioned Rider's shout. The intense cold of the hills had done more than clothe the trees with ice, it had weighed them down with a heavy burden of frozen snow so their heads sagged, and stiffened in a drooping position. One tall pine had been unable to take the weight and as the car drove towards it there was a loud cracking noise, sharp as a pistol shot before it swayed and lurched and began to lean towards the road. Instinctively Rider had braked, seeing it; his later reaction, a surge of speed, had been brought about by the realization that the tree was going to crash across the road. They could be barred from the spillway dam by the fallen timber, so he drove the car at top speed for the ridge and the pine lurched, swung towards them, and its head dropped for the roadway with a sudden terrifying speed.

Ben yelled a warning for they were not going to get past the tree in time but his shout was frozen in his throat as there was a tremendous flash that lit up the whole of the ridge and cast deep shadows among the trees. The car roared past and under the bouncing pine and Ben realized that the tree had struck the ice-covered wires; it was hanging there, momentarily, and the car was past and away but as he glanced back through the rear window Ben saw the second violent burst of illumination as the telephone wires gave way and the tree sliced through the power lines to crash down, straddling the road blackly, effectively cutting off the route to Fenokee, some miles below.

'Hell, you left that late!'

'We made it, didn't we?'

And ahead of them they saw the lights of the spillway dam. Whatever use the power lines had been they did not seem to have affected the lights at the dam, but Ben guessed that the construction site would have generating equipment which was probably kept on automatic switch in the event of a power failure from the lines. Such procedures were necessary up here in the hills where damage in the intense cold was quite possible and lines could come down fairly regularly during the winter months.

They drove up towards the gorge and the dam towered above them, sealing the V-shape of the cut in the hills and twisting the river across to the right in a mill-race that effectively prevented a heavy build-up of ice. Even so, heavy freezing had occurred along the shoreline and long tongues of ice crept out into the middle of the river, clinging to rocks and growing, expanding beyond them until they found new footholds upon which they could seize and continue their spanning of the river. The central channel was only feet wide, and as they drove past the banks Ben guessed that by morning the whole of the river surface could well be ice-bound.

They emerged at the top of the hill from under the trees and drove straight on to the edge of the dam. They saw no workmen; the damhead seemed virtually deserted, though there were lights across by the new section of the dam, and as Rider stopped the car engine they could hear the rumble of drilling equipment in the distance. Seth Davis's car was parked beside the control centre and it was here that Rider left him. They got out and Ben ran up the steps of the control centre, slipping twice as he went. Rider followed more cautiously, wary of the thick black ice that encrusted the steps and handrails in a smooth cold sheet.

Ben opened the door of the control house and Rider followed him in. The great bank of electrical equipment faced them sombrely; the small radio room beyond presented a closed door to them and Ben marched across and flung open the door without ceremony. A startled operator swung his head to look at him. Ben opened his mouth to speak but Rider put a hand on his shoulder.

'Wait.'

Ben turned, and he too heard the steps on the stairs outside the control house. Next moment the door opened and Seth Davis entered the room. Ben quietly closed the door of the radio room behind him and faced Davis as the man stared at him and Rider with a slack-jawed expression.

'Ben! What the hell are you–'

His expression changed as the words died on his lips. He flickered a glance towards Rider and tried to speak again but no words came. Rider moved forward slowly and reached for the door behind Davis, closing it quietly as Davis stepped to one side nervously. He found his tongue again at last.

'What … what's the matter? What do you want?'

'Just a talk,' Ben said grimly. 'Just a quiet talk about something that happened seven years ago.'

2

The face that emerged from the radio room was young, with tousled hair and an anxious expression. He looked around at the three silent men.

'All right, Mr Davis?'

Seth Davis stood stiffly, his glance locked with Ben's. He was pale, and his breathing was shallow and quick. Ben stared at him and made no attempt to hide the cold anger he felt. His silence made it clear to Davis that he was not going to be sidetracked, by the young operator or anyone else.

'It's … it's all right, Joe. Leave us.'

The troubled operator closed the door and Rider shifted lazily to lean against the wall.

'That was sensible,' he said.

'I don't know what you want,' Seth Davis said urgently to Ben, 'but this is a hell of a time to start talking! I can't afford to talk about … about Joanna with you now, because we're in a hell of a lot of trouble up here and–'

'The trouble you're in has nothing to do with the dam,' Ben cut in. 'I want to know about Joanna, and you're going to talk about her whether you like it or not! I want to know about Joanna and Philip Starling and I want to know what happened that night she died!'

'Philip Starling – you can't know … you … I don't know what you mean! How can I tell you–'

He spun anxiously on his heel as though to walk back towards the door but Rider came up from the wall and stood facing him with his arms dangling at his sides. He looked more than capable of dealing with the situation, and Davis was a worried man. He waved the book he carried in his hands, a gesture of desperation.

'Please, Ben, can't we leave this until later?

I got enough trouble on my hands right now to–'

'You introduced them didn't you, you arranged that they should meet, Joanna and Philip Starling?'

'Arrange, no, hell I didn't arrange nothin'! He just met her at the house one day and … look, Ben, for God's sake!'

Ben stepped forward, his head lowered like an angry bull. He clenched his fists and Rider stood watchfully at Davis's shoulder.

'*I want to know!*' Ben snarled, and Davis shuddered. He seemed to have lost all the control he had previously possessed; perhaps it was the shock of seeing Ben here at all when he had thought him thousands of miles away; perhaps it was the shock of being questioned like this when he had other worries on his mind. Whatever the reason, he had lost his capacity to fight, and he was badly scared. He shook his head.

'All right, I introduced them, but that was all! The rest of it–'

'Tell me the rest of it!'

'There wasn't any more. I swear–'

'Joanna did phone that day didn't she? And you took the call!'

'What? How can you know – all right, all right, she did phone and I did take the call and Mary was out and didn't know about it. Joanna said she was stuck out at Valley Fork, in a drift, so I said I'd go out and bring her in, but then Philip arrived and we went off in his car. When we reached Valley Fork we found that she'd got the car dug out by a garage mechanic, but he had to free a buckled fender so we went into town in Philip's car and got us a meal…'

His voice died away. Ben gritted his teeth.

'Were they having an affair?'

Davis jumped like a startled rabbit. He looked away from Ben, glared at the book in his hands and shook his head woodenly.

'No. What the hell you mean by that? They hardly knew each other.'

'Don't lie to me, Davis. I want the truth. We can prove that Joanna had … had sexual intercourse not long before she died!'

Davis's eyes were startled and his voice displayed a tremor of panic.

'I don't know a thing about that, honest, Ben, you have to believe me, I don't–'

'What happened that evening? Was it you, or Starling, or did you both rape her?'

'Rape? What do you say rape for? I had nothing to do with what happened!'

'What did happen?'

Davis lurched around suddenly in desperation, flailing his arm helplessly.

'I don't know. Hell, nothing happened, we just went back for the car and then Philip asked me to drive and he got to talking with Joanna and she seemed kinda depressed and lonely or somethin' and he suggested they go out together for a drink and a meal that evening and that was that. She agreed, asked me to phone Mary to tell her–'

'But you didn't!'

'I… No, I didn't, I just … well, she didn't know Joanna was there and Starling said… Starling said not to bother.'

'*And?*'

'And we went to a club. Hell, I didn't know what was happening, Ben, or what he intended. I guess he wanted her, but I didn't know what was going on! We'd smoked some reefers at college and I didn't know that Philip still used them – well, at the club he persuaded Joanna to try one, or maybe she didn't even know what it was all about, but suddenly there we were, and it was late, and we'd been drinking and she was high, and Philip tossed me the keys of his car and told me to take it back to town for him.'

'And you did just that, I suppose!'

'Yes.'

'And Joanna?'

'The two of them went off in her car, Philip driving.'

Davis had changed. A truculence had come into his voice and he was staring sullenly at Ben. His earlier weakness was evaporating and he was regaining control of himself as his panic subsided. He gritted his teeth, and the grinding sound was harsh in the sudden silence.

'That's all I know about it. All right, she was found dead of exposure in the valley. I know nothin' about that, or about anythin' that happened between her and Philip. I didn't enquire.'

'The price of your lack of interest being the spillway dam?' Ben asked angrily, but Davis had no time to answer. The door opened, there was a swirl of cold air, and three men walked into the control centre. Rider moved back towards Ben as Davis spun on his heel and there in the doorway stood Grant Starling. Behind him was a man in a green helmet whom Ben had never seen before. The third man, entering the room behind the others and beating his arms against his side, was Edward Rose. His arms stopped their movement as he caught sight of Ben and Rider, and a gleam of utter malevolence shot from his eyes. Starling was staring at the two men with his mouth open.

'You … what's your name … South – what the hell are you doing here?'

Without waiting for a reply he turned his craggy head towards Rose and bellowed, 'What the hell is this man doing here? I thought I told you to get him out of my hair?'

Rose's face was lined with anger and mingled hate as he glared at Ben but he made no reply. Ben answered for him.

'He tried to frighten me off. He got Cornelius to break his contract with me, thinking it would keep me quiet. But it doesn't work, Starling, because I know too much, about you and your son, and now I've got the proof to back it up.'

'He's crazy, Mr Starling,' Davis interrupted swiftly, 'he's got some crazy ideas–'

'The hell with him and his ideas!' Grant Starling cut Davis short with a peremptory gesture. 'We've got more to worry about than a broken businessman with ideas about a shakedown! I've told you once, South, I don't scare, or pay out! So get the hell out of here, while you can, or you'll get wheeled out in a dump truck!'

He strode past, his shoulder striking Ben's contemptuously as he thrust past towards the window. He was motioning to Davis as he walked, obviously regarding his brief interview with Ben already over.

'Well, Davis, what were the readings?'

Rose came forward, glancing sideways at Rider, and Davis cast a nervous look in Ben's direction before turning to answer Starling.

'They've made the borings on the surface and it shows about two or two and a half feet of crystal ice packed on the surface.'

'And below that?'

Davis licked his lips.

'Maybe thirty feet of loose pack ice.'

'Hell's bells!' Starling glowered at Davis then swung around, catching sight again of Ben and Rider. He snarled at Rose. 'Get these two characters out of here before I throw them out myself.'

'Starling–' began Ben menacingly but the craggy construction man was already bawling through to the radio room.

'Have you got through to Fairmont yet? Hey, you in there!'

As the young operator opened the door and looked out Rose touched Ben on the arm. His face was grim.

'You and your companion had better get out of here. You realize you're trespassing, and you're not welcome.'

Ben shook off the arm and said fiercely,

'You don't get rid of me just like that, Rose. I've got questions to ask of Starling, and I mean to get the answers.'

'The hell you say you can't get through!' Starling was yelling at the unfortunate operator. 'What hell is with everybody around here! There's three miles of ice blocking the lake solid, there's only a skeleton staff up here because some fool of an engineer decides to get married in the middle of winter, there's some doubt about the strength of the inner skin of the walls of the dam, and now you tell me you can't get through to Fairmont!'

'It wasn't only the power line that must have been cut,' the operator complained with a show of spirit. 'As soon as that went off our emergency supply came on but the phone lines are down too, they must be!'

'Then get them fixed!'

Davis intervened nervously.

'But the fault could be anywhere along seven miles or more of line, sir. We'll never find it tonight!'

Starling was glaring contemptuously at the contractor when Rider drawled,

'In fact, the line is down about two miles along the track. A tree, fallen across the road. Even if you got the line fixed you'd have to clear the track before you could get anyone up here. I presume that's what you want, more men up here.'

Grant Starling's face was grim.

'Rose, I told you to get these two out.'

'They're on the way, Mr Starling.' There was a determined edge to Rose's tone and he was motioning towards the helmeted man. 'Stevens, if they're not out of here in ten seconds I want you to go down to the dam and collect half a dozen men to throw these two off the site.'

'That'll give us time to have our say,' Ben remarked coldly. 'Starling, we've come up here because we've got most of the answers to our questions but we want confirmation. I've already dragged out of Davis the fact that my wife—'

'The hell with your wife! Get this straight, South, I'm not interested in your dead wife, and I'm not interested in your questions! You try to malign my son and I'll see you in

251

a box! Right now all I want is to get you out of my hair, because Davis has allowed this ice to block his spillway and seize up the new cofferdam. Within hours the pressure of that ice is likely to break the cofferdam, and perhaps thrust a fist right through those dam walls. There'll be a flood of ice and water over that breach that will make another year's work necessary and if it does break through it's going to tear the guts out of the hillside on its way down to Fenokee. And when it hits Fenokee there's going to be one hell of a smash! So don't talk to me about your smear campaign, don't bother me with snide cracks about what my son did or didn't do, don't try to push me towards a shakedown because it won't work that way! Now get the hell out of here! Stevens, you heard what Mr Rose said! Ten seconds!'

He turned his suffused face away and glared at Davis.

'Well, what the hell are you going to do about this ice?'

'I don't know! The blasters are down at Carson's stag in Fairmont, and we've got no one who is capable of handling dynamite!'

Ben was still burning with anger but he found Davis's words curious. In spite of his anger, and in spite of the fact that his errand here was one of antagonism towards Davis and Starling, he was nevertheless appreciative of the problem that faced them, and

Davis's suggested solution puzzled him.

'Dynamite?' he asked. 'What are you going to do with dynamite?'

Starling balled two huge fists and turned as though to roar at Ben. Rider moved forward unobtrusively, taking up a better defensive position, but Davis answered quickly, and snappily.

'What do you think we'll do with it? That ice is blocking the lake, if we don't break it up it'll destroy the last cofferdam and breach the dam walls! There's only one way to break it and that's with dynamite!'

'How are you going to blow it? And where'll you fuse it? You're crazy, Seth!'

'We can't do a dam thing with it until the blasters get here, and they'll know how to work it!'

Ben shook his head angrily. He had almost forgotten his quarrel with Seth Davis and Grant Starling as he saw the incompetence with which he was faced.

'Don't be stupid! To start with, the blasters aren't here; it would take them two hours to get here; you'd have to clear that tree before you could even get a message to them; and when they got here they'd tell you they couldn't blast that ice! They couldn't because all they'd do is tear a hole in it, which would just freeze over again, and how would that relieve the pressure on the dam walls?'

'They could blast near the dam!'

253

'And do the job that you fear the ice will do – knock a hole in the dam itself! This is stupid, Seth, this isn't the way to do it!'

The exchange between the two men had caught Grant Starling's interest. There was a speculative gleam in his eye as he stared at Ben South. The surveyor saw Rose nod towards Stevens and the helmeted engineer started for the door but Starling raised an arm and stopped him.

'Wait! All right, *Mr* South! Tell me this, just what does an English surveyor know about working a dam in Canada?'

Ben glared contemptuously at the man who had covered up his son's misdeeds. He was tempted to let them get on with it themselves, and make fools of themselves, blow a hole in their dam, destroy Fenokee and then he'd laugh at them. But he couldn't do it.

'Before I qualified in England,' he said stiffly, 'I was a surveyor in Canada. I worked in the river valleys in Alberta, and I spent a few years on the Seaway.'

'And that qualifies you to tell Davis he's wrong?'

'I know he's wrong. This isn't a new problem, and if you'd worked with dams in temperatures below zero you'd know how to handle this too.'

'All right, Mr Qualified Surveyor South, initiate the uninitiated!'

They were all standing there staring at

him and he made them wait, because of the sneer in Starling's tones. At last he said,

'If Carson were here he'd know what to do, Starling. But all we have is the big executives, the characters who know how to handle money and people, and who know how to run men's lives and destroy men too; who know how to play the power game but can't face a practical problem for what it is. You, and Rose, and Davis too, you're all so preoccupied with your power games that you've forgotten the basic principles that you must have known as a child!'

'You say this problem is a simple one?'

Davis tone rasped in the tense air of the control room. Ben nodded coldly.

'Ever seen a child in a bathtub. Playing with the water, making it run back and forth? Move your hand at the right speed in a bathtub and you can rock the water to a regular tempo.'

'This is a dam not a bathtub!'

'But the principle is the same! What's a dam if it's not a bathtub, except that it's measured in miles instead of inches, and there's a flowing channel pouring water into it!'

Davis shook his head disgustedly but Starling waved him to remain silent. He glared at Ben.

'Time's short,' he growled. 'That dam could burst within an hour, maybe less. Let's hear what this man has to say.'

'There's no hand big enough to rock this dam water,' Davis insisted truculently.

'But you've got sluice gates!'

Silence fell, and Rider stirred restlessly behind Ben. Rose was biting his thumbnail, his eyes never leaving the surveyor's face, and the engineer at the door was listening in fascination.

'Instead of a hand, you use your sluice gates. You've got four gates. What you must do is close two of those gates as rapidly as you can, leaving the other two open. Those closed gates will back up perhaps a third of the flow into the dam.'

'What then?' Davis sneered.

'Then you open the gates again; that'll pull extra water down through the dam.'

'I don't see what the hell that's going to do!'

'Wait, hear the man out.' Grant Starling's tone was peremptory as he listened to Ben with a frown on his face.

'If you open those gates swiftly, and close them again, then repeat the manoeuvre what'll happen? The closing of the gates will bring water rolling forward and smashing against the dam wall. The water will roll back up into the lake under the ice because there's no way out for it. While it's surging back you're opening the gates again, and that'll draw water down into the dam. The water drawn down meets the surge tearing back up into the lake itself. The effect of it all will be just like the hand in the bathtub – you'll set up a turbulent motion under the surface, and it'll smash the ice.'

'It's crazy!'

'It'll work. The first drawdown will suck water from under the ice, the pack ice will start to move and waves will run under the ice, to smash against the wall when the gates close, run and meet the next rush of water drawn down by the reopening of the gates. Open and close those gates in rhythm and that ice will break.'

Davis shook his head obstinately.

The ice is two feet thick!'

'And there's thirty feet of loose ice underneath it. I know. I heard you first time. But I tell you it'll break.'

'I still think all we can do is dynamite it.'

'Shaddup, Davis.' Grant Starling spoke decisively. 'South makes sense in theory. Let's see what happens in practice.'

'You mean you're going to try it?'

'What the hell else can we do? The pressure's building on those walls and I don't aim to see Fenokee go smash because you think we should wait for a repaired phone line, and dynamiters who might blow a hole in the dam anyway! Stevens, get those sluice gates open! South, which ones for the most effect?'

Ben shrugged.

'The two centre ones, I reckon.'

Stevens moved to the controls and the

others watched him silently. He glanced towards Ben and then operated both gates simultaneously.

'That's full throttle,' he said quietly.

They waited and the hum of the machinery was the only sound apart from the whistle of the wind which had begun to rise and whip around the control room. Grant Starling stared out through the frosted windows towards the mass of the dam, a white, vague sheet spreading across their entire field of vision and merging finally with a grey-black sky.

'Full open,' Stevens reported.

'Give it thirty seconds.'

Ben watched them tick away and then nodded to Stevens. The engineer slammed the controls again, together. Davis cleared his throat nervously and Rider shuffled behind Ben's back. The whine of the wind rose, changing in speed and force. There was a light pattering sound against the class of the windows, flying ice, wind-borne, needle-sharp.

'Closed.'

'Open them again.'

'Straight away?'

'Straight away.'

'Away she goes!'

Grant Starling lurched away from the window to face Ben. Rose moved over beside him, his book-keeper's eyes fixed on Ben, his lean frame slightly stooping, his mouth set in a grim line. Starling glanced at him thoughtfully then said to Ben,

'How many times do you reckon we go through this procedure?'

'Till the ice breaks up.'

'*If* it breaks up!'

'It will. Three times maybe, and it'll start to break when we close the gates the third time, I reckon.'

'There'll be a hell of a flood down through the sluices when it does go.'

'A few thousand tons of ice will go down from the spillway, but it's better down below than here, because if these walls go there'll be a hell of a lot more than that pounding down to Fenokee.'

There was a speculative look in Starling's eye and when he spoke again there was a certain grudging respect in his tone.

'You think you're a pretty smart feller, South ... and maybe you are. We'll see, when and if that pack ice moves out.'

Rose spoke for the first time for several minutes.

'There's only one way we'll know if the ice breaks up – we go down to see it.'

Starling nodded.

'Right. Come on down, South, and let's see if your expertise stands you in good stead.'

'Full open, and thirty seconds to go,' Stevens intoned, and Ben pulled the collar of his coat up around his ears.

'Let's go,' he said to Starling and stood aside as the tall craggy man made for the door. Starling smiled grimly as he passed Ben and there was an enigmatic quality about that smile that brought Ben's mind back to the immediate reason for his visit to the spillway dam. He had come to question Davis, and Starling, about the death of his wife, but he had hardly thought about it for some minutes. Instead, he was pitting his wits and knowledge alongside Starling to fight the vast enemy outside the control house, the solid grinding mass of ice that threatened the biggest project Canada had seen for years, since the Seaway. He shoved his hands into his gloves and followed Starling out into the bitter cold on the platform of the control house.

The evening had changed in character. Where the moon had ridden high, drifting among storm clouds, there was now just a vast blank greyness and as Ben lifted his face he could feel the sharp sting of the minute crystals of ice driven through the air by the biting wind. He turned his back, averted his face and tried to look around at the dam site but the lights were only pale glimmers on the near wall; the hutments were blotted out by the driving ice spicules which effectively limited vision to a matter of yards.

Rider was at his shoulder.

'You going to be all right?'

His voice was lifted by the wind, tossed around the platform, and Starling's head rose from his chest, to stare blankly at the two of them standing there. Ben nodded, and stepped aside to make way for Rose as he came out, well muffled.

'You stay up here,' he said in a low tone to Rider, then waited until Rose had passed before he continued. 'I don't want Seth moving out while I'm out here with Starling.'

'Good enough. Damn sight warmer inside anyway!'

Rider went back in and closed the door. Ben moved towards the steps and saw Rose below, wielding a short crowbar, attacking the steps and the guide-rail with sharp blows.

'He's trying to clear some of the ice – make it safer going down,' Starling explained.

'Stop it!' bawled Ben above the howl of the wind. 'You'll snap either the rail or the crowbar – in this temperature the metal will be brittle.'

Even as he spoke the crowbar struck the guide-rail again and a piece flew from its end, to drop into the darkness below. Rose ceased his activity and stared up silently towards the two men above. Grant Starling looked at Ben, and the surveyor motioned for Starling to go ahead, Starling did so with a grim smile, and Ben followed him down the steps.

They moved down across the head of the dam, making for the wall and the wind whistled around them, dragging and tearing at their clothing, hurling the sharp ice particles against the exposed skin of their faces, and there was no one else near them. They could have been completely alone in this cold, whistling world and there were only the lights glowing mistily in the dimness to show that men and warmth awaited them above. The skeleton staff still up at the spillway would be at the far end of the dam awaiting instructions; they had carried out the boring, but they wouldn't know about the new activity. The thought made Ben realize that they ought to make sure there was no one in danger near the sluice gates. He mentioned it to Starling.

'Rose, get back up to the control house and make sure everyone's clear – though it's pretty certain they are, because there's no reason why anyone should be down on those gates. But just in case any of the drillers are still on the ice, get them the hell out of there.'

Rose nodded silently, and vanished towards the control house steps. Ben and Starling walked towards the wall of the dam and stood there, staring out across the dam. They could see the ice glowing below them, a solid, unmoving pack of white iron, spreading out across from them into the darkness upstream and across the long curve of the dam. The two men stood at the wall, staring down, and Grant Starling suddenly said in a quiet voice,

'You been buggin' me, South.'

And Ben realized that they were alone in the howling void above the dam.

3

The wall of the dam was in front of him, and the guide-rail was against his hand. Below in the darkness Ben could just make out a catwalk, a temporary structure that had been slung there to provide an access to the ice. It must have been by way of this catwalk that the workmen had got down to undertake the drilling and the checks on the wall itself. There was no one down there now. Ben raised his arm, shielding his face against the biting spicules and squinted at the craggy old man standing at his side.

'That's right, Starling, I been bugging you.'

'So what do you want?'

'I told you. The truth.'

'I thought you were trying for a shake-down.'

'That's what you wanted it to be – you wanted to hear no criticism of your son.'

Starling's face was averted. He leaned against the wall, peering out over the surface of the lake, silently. After a while he said,

'No sign of this damned ice moving.' His voice was harsh and gritty. 'This blasted dam … if I'd've seen the construction details in the first instance I'd never have passed them. It comes of delegating, you know that, South? This kind of construction technique hasn't been sounded out, not tested, but my people allow it to go through–'

'Yes. I wondered about it myself.'

'You been here before?'

'Months back. I almost got killed, down below.'

Starling stared at him for a moment and then squared his shoulders, hunching into his coat decisively.

'All right. Seems to me you got things to say. And maybe I was wrong, maybe this is no shakedown. You say you want the truth. About what? My son? Your wife? Me? I don't know, South – I've revised my opinion of you somewhat this evening, I've seen you showing some hard sense and I know you've been a construction man and that says a lot in my book. But I don't know what you want.'

'Your son knew my wife. He took her out the night she died. I want to know what happened.'

'I know nothing of this. You say you can prove it so why come to me?'

'Because you paid for the seven-year silence!'

Grant Starling was tall, taller than Ben and though he was sixty he was a man of whipcord and steel.

'What the hell do you mean by that?'

'You can't bluff me out of this, Starling. I

can prove it. I can prove you paid Joe Pearl, and Dr Nebbia, and probably Durrance too, to maintain silence about your son and my wife.'

Starling's eyes were narrowed against the wind, but Ben thought he could see the hard gleam in them.

'I don't know what the hell you're talking about! I've never heard of these men!'

'They gave perjured evidence at the inquest into my wife's death; Pearl got a cheque from you, Nebbia got paid through one of your companies; Durrance, well, he probably got paid the same way but ended up under a car. Who did you pay to drive that car, Starling?'

'You're getting wilder and wilder! You're trying to fix more than bribery on me now! You say you've got evidence but I don't see how, and like I said, I don't even know these people! And at the time concerned–'

'So you know the time!'

Starling paused, then said coldly,

'After your visit to me I got Rose to check it out. Yes, I know the time it happened. During that period I was undergoing treatment for a broken thigh. I just wasn't around to undertake any of the nonsense you mention.'

'I suppose you own the nursing home too,' Ben sneered. 'That alibi will be easy to fix!'

'I need no alibi because I don't even know

what you're talking about. I got Rose to check the story of your wife's death and the possible implication of my son and he came up with a negative on the latter and a coroner's verdict on the first. The story you shoot me about these men – I just don't know what you're talking about.'

There was a ring of sincerity in Starling's voice that puzzled Ben. But he had the evidence of Joe Pearl's notes, and Nebbia's testimony. Grimly, he said.

'I can't accept that, Starling. Pearl got a cheque signed by you.'

'You're crazy – he can't have!'

'And Dr Nebbia was paid by a man in your employ.'

'The hell with that! Who paid him?'

'A man called Haggett. A lawyer who works for one of your companies.'

'Haggett? Who the hell ... did you say Haggett?'

Starling was leaning forward, his face creased in a frown but suddenly his eyes were flickering past Ben, widening with relief.

Ben turned, aware of a dark movement among the swirl of ice and snow in the air above the dam and he saw the lean figure of Edward Rose materialize out of the darkness. He stood a few feet away from them, quietly, his hands by his sides, staring at them.

'I tried to tell you, warn you, Mr Starling, that you shouldn't have any truck with this

266

man South.'

'And I told you to get him off my back, but he's here, so let's get this finished with once and for all.'

Rose peered towards Ben through the driving snow.

'I thought Cornelius breaking your contract would make you concentrate on other things, South. You've made a mistake, pursuing this.'

'No,' Ben shouted, 'it's Starling who made the mistake trying to hush things up by getting Haggett to pay–'

'The hell with this!' Grant Starling gesticulated violently towards Rose. 'South reckons that Haggett paid some people to give perjured evidence and that *I* paid someone called Pearl to do the same. Now what the hell is it all about?'

Rose turned his lean face towards Starling; in the dimness no expression could be made out, his face was a blur, a blank nonentity, unreadable.

'It's all true, of course. Haggett *did* pay Durrance and Dr Nebbia. And *you* paid Joe Pearl.'

'Rose! Are you crazy? What are you trying to say?'

'I'm not surprised you don't remember signing your cheque for Joe Pearl, of course. After all, Philip brought it to you when you were at the nursing home, telling you it was for an educational charity and that he'd write in the name of the treasurer later. You signed like a lamb ... you always trusted Philip, so pathetically.'

'Philip ... are you trying to say *Philip* paid Pearl with a cheque signed by me, and arranged for Haggett to pay the others?'

Rose laughed, an unpleasant sound that razored against the howling wind and was tossed up to the sky an the darkness.

'Can't you believe that of Philip? Can't you believe it of the swindling young bastard? You, the model father, bringing your son up in a tough school, making him hard and independent! Didn't you know he bribed his way through college, always sought the easy way out, used money to buy what he wanted?'

There was only the wild scream of the wind about them. Ben and Grant Starling stood as though turned to stone, staring at the lean vicious figure facing them. Rose was laughing again, laughing at Grant Starling's shock.

'You never knew what he was like, *Mr* Starling! But I knew! As you gave me more and more responsibility in the organization I saw him grow up and I knew that in a few years he'd take your place and that I'd have to answer to him – that weakling! So I did all I could to make him dependent on me – I encouraged his excesses behind your back, I used him, I bought him! And you stayed in a dream world. Why, you even thought that he died a *hero!* How gullible can you get? There were no heroics for Philip Starling – both he and the pilot were killed instantly in that crash!'

'Rose!' Starling was starting forward, one arm raised, but Edward Rose moved swiftly and Starling stopped. Ben stared at Rose; the man was still holding the broken crowbar he had carried earlier and now it was raised menacingly.

'What the hell is all this about!' Grant Starling snarled.

'Don't push me, Starling! I tried to keep you two apart, but it's too late now!'

'What the hell are you playing at?' Starling shouted in frustration.

'Oh, it's a game all right! The biggest! Do you think I was prepared to run the damned organization for you and take a salary and say thank you very much? I used your son as a means to get more power in the company but I had other ideas too – and the biggest was the Fenokee Project!'

'What's the project got to do with this?'

'Everything! I knew Starling Enterprises would fail to convince the government that the Project should be mounted so I approached Senator Roberts and together we hammered out a deal. He agreed to use his considerable political influence to get

American backing if I swung it so that a large slice of the finance would come back to him. Between us we hatched a deal that was to make us rich. And then your stupid son nearly blew it!'

Rose shook the crowbar angrily; his own words made him shake with spasmodic fury at the recollections they brought back.

'It was essential that no link be established between Roberts and me before the Project was mooted. We were up at the lodge with Haggett, cooking the final details, when your blasted son walked in, high as a kite, and introduced that damned girl to us as though it were a vicarage tea party! Roberts went crazy and lit out as fast as he could but I thought we could still swing it until next morning. The girl had been hopped-up too, she couldn't have known what was happening, and she came out of that bedroom like she was mad, screaming, yelling rape! Haggett and I tried to calm her down but it was no good. She threatened all sorts of things! I couldn't be sure that she'd even remember Roberts was there but I knew sure as hell that if she brought charges against Philip, with a drugs rap and rape involved there'd be a close police investigation that would inevitably lead to Roberts's presence at the lodge being known. And my deal with him would be blow sky-high! I couldn't take that!'

'You killed Joanna!'

'It would have meant the end of the Fenokee deal! Haggett was still trying to calm her when I knew what had to be done. I went out to her car and I fixed her brakes. She wanted to phone for assistance at the lodge but we stopped that and she drove away about midday. I hoped she'd plough into the trees and get killed but it didn't quite work that way. No matter. She ended up dead, in the snow, and we were clear!'

'You killed my wife!'

'And I was safe, until *you* started shoving your nose in! Why the hell couldn't you leave things alone? Why did you have to push things, why didn't you listen when I warned you? Well, it's too damn late now!'

Grant Starling stood tall, clenching his fists. He was in a towering rage, now that the first drenching shock of the truth about his son was over.

'Rose, you better–'

Edward Rose raised the crowbar and shook it.

'And you! Didn't I tell you to have no truck with South? Didn't I warn you that he'd mean trouble if you didn't allow me to deal with him? Well, you didn't listen, damn you, and now–'

Starling bellowed and began to lurch forward only to stop short as from behind him there came a loud cracking noise, sharp as a whiplash above the howl of the wind.

271

Instinctively, and in spite of the menace of Rose both Starling and Ben looked back, startled, towards the white mass of ice beyond the dam wall and heard another explosive cracking sound, followed by a slow grinding sound.

The ice was breaking up.

It should have sent excitement boiling up inside them but there was no time. Ben heard Starling's warning and half-turned but it was too late. He caught a brief glimpse of something black whirring for his head and he ducked. Next moment he felt a numbing blow on his shoulder, he staggered sideways and felt the edge of the dam wall bite against his ribs. Starling shouted again but Ben was toppling over the rail, falling towards the white grinding mass that reached up to him coldly from the darkness.

Then something hit him hard in the pit of his stomach.

4

They were words in a dream, distant, attenuated, spoken through the whine of an icy wind that seared into his brain and numbed it into semi-consciousness. A band of pain throbbed across his stomach and his cheek was burning but it was several seconds before Ben realized where he was or what had happened. Seconds, and yet they ticked away with a slowness that seemed to represent aeons to Ben, as he lay sprawled on the catwalk fifteen feet below the dam wall and suspended, rocking, some thirty feet above the grinding mass of ice on the surface of the dam.

His head ached but his brain cleared slowly, and he realized that the blow which had struck his shoulder had also knocked him lurching against the dam wall and the rail so that he fell over. But he'd been lucky; the catwalk had lain below and its rail had doubled him up, a harsh blow across his stomach; now he was lying on the catwalk itself with his exposed cheek freezing to the metal of the step. He turned, gingerly, and felt the tear of skin then the stiff numbness of his exposed face; he rose, dragging himself to his knees and looked upwards but saw nothing. The words still whirled down to him from the sky, however, ghostly words caught in freak eddies of the wind, clearer to him on the catwalk than perhaps they were to the their recipient above. The voice he could hardly recognize; the vicious import he could, and it caused him to stagger to his feet.

'...your damned son ... almost ruined everything! I'd planned ... and then in he walked and Roberts was there ... what else could I do ... easy enough with Pearl because he was a little man and poor...

Durrance was a greedy fool. But don't talk to me about your precious Philip ... corrupted, but what the hell would you know about it? You gave up the responsibility years ago ... and now with the congressional enquiry in progress things are too close and South ... you've got to follow him, Starling, there's no choice for me but...'

Ben staggered as the wind buffeted him where he stood just below the top of the wall on the swinging catwalk. Above him he could see the dark shape of Grant Starling in semi-profile, one hand braced against the wall, one raised in a futile gesture of mixed defiance and defence. Needles of ice stung Ben's face as he peered upwards past Starling and saw the crouching black figure of his assailant. Edward Rose stood huddled in his coat, and Ben could not make out his features but the crowbar was still in his hand, and he was threatening Starling. The construction tycoon was shouting something, incomprehensible words that were an amalgam of fury and defiance and aggression but they were cut short as the man facing him surged forward in a long leap, swinging the weapon he carried and Grant Starling was staggering back against the wall as Ben had done, one hand raised, protecting his head.

Ben lurched his way upwards, desperately, on the catwalk and it began to swing violently so that he slipped and fell to his knees. He glanced upwards again and through the wind and ice drift saw Starling's broad back against the wall and the other man pressing against his throat. Ben glanced around in desperation, hanging on to the ice-sheathed rail. The catwalk ran in a curving ascent twenty yards beyond the struggling couple before it reached the top of the wall and Ben knew that if he tried to get along there Starling might well be thrust over the edge before he could make it. The two men were ten or twelve feet above him, out of reach, but he was unobserved. He looked around desperately, and saw the pinning of the catwalk to the wall of the dam, strong linchpins, supporting the weight of the catwalk along twenty feet intervals. He grabbed at the pin, tugged at it, and it held firmly. He put one foot on the rail of the catwalk and it lurched but the hand he kept on the pin was rock steady and he pulled himself upwards, taking the weight on his left foot until he was standing, dragging one arm forward and feeling the deadening pain of his shoulder, lifting his right foot until he was up to the pin, standing above and on it and spread-eagled to the wall like a fly, his arms wide, his head just eighteen inches below the rim of the wall.

There were no words now. Grant Starling's head was close to Ben's own for that few brief seconds, and in that time Ben was able to see Starling's chin being forced upwards, the hood falling back from Starling's coat, the iron, bar, gripped fiercely in the gloved hands of Edward Rose, thrust against Starling's throat. Eighteen inches; the contorted features of Starling's employee; the wind buffeting at Ben as he raised one hand, releasing the pressure he had been maintaining on the wall; Starling sliding sideways and Ben's fingers reaching for the shoulder of Rose's coat as he was pressed to the wall.

The cloth was under his hand. Ben grabbed at it, wound his fingers into it and felt the jerk, the start of surprise from Rose. He could see Rose's wild eyes staring into his unbelievingly, and then Rose was dragging backwards, trying to pull himself free.

He had reckoned without Starling. The man came up from under the pressure of the crowbar, swinging Rose forward violently, and Rose now found himself with Ben's fierce grip clutching at his shoulder. He again tried to break free and in furious desperation Ben threw up his other hand and clutched, hung on to Edward Rose with both hands swinging free from the wall. And with wild terror Ben realized that he was consigning himself to a backbreaking fall to the ice. As Starling suddenly tore away from the throttling constraint of the crowbar Rose was off balance and dragged by the weight of Ben's body, with no purchase to take it; he let out a terrified cry, and came over the edge of the wall towards Ben.

It was over in a second. Suddenly Ben was no longer suspended, and Rose was flying over his head as Ben's fingers were torn loose from his grip on Rose's coat. Ben's foot struck the catwalk, and the force of the blow held him for a brief split second, long enough for Rose's screaming face to be thrust out and above him and the man's body to strike Ben downwards, against the rail of the catwalk before hurtling outwards and away towards the ice. Ben lay sprawled, winded, on the steps of the catwalk and above the grinding of the ice below he heard the solid thud as Rose struck the hard surface.

Then there was only the howl of the wind.

Ben lay still, and stared downwards at the surface of the ice and the still black figure that was Rose. The man was at least unconscious; at worst, his neck or his back would be broken by the fall. A tremor shook the catwalk, a clanging noise, feet descending hurriedly. Starling was coming down. Moments later a hand shook Ben, grabbing his shoulders, and he felt pain shoot through his arm.

'South! Are you...' Starling was gasping breathlessly, and the wind plucked the words from his mouth almost before he could utter them. 'Are you all right?'

Ben nodded slowly.

'Help me up. He ... he...'

'Crazy,' Starling muttered as he put an

arm under Ben's shoulder. 'He went berserk, with that bar...'

'We'll have to get him up. He may ... may still be alive.'

'Get you up first, off this catwalk.'

Half-supporting each other, the two men staggered up the icy catwalk, buffeted by the howling wind, stung by the vicious driving ice particles until they reached the top of the dam wall, and climbed over thankfully. They moved back along the top of the dam until they were directly above the figure on the ice. Through the flurry of ice spicules Ben could see the dark figure move slightly, slowly, as though emerging from unconsciousness.

'He's alive, Starling, get someone from the control tower. Get them down here, we're neither of us in a condition to do...'

He stopped talking. He felt Grant Starling stiffen beside him as they both watched. Edward Rose was moving, rising to one knee, slowly, like an old man tired with life. His face looked up, a pale blur in the dimness, and he was lifting one hand as though asking for assistance. But both men on the dam could hear the cracking, the sound of ice breaking up, and they both saw the dark finger widening, slipping along the whiteness towards Rose. The waves set up by the opening and closing of the sluice gates had done their work, the ice was breaking up, and floes forty and fifty feet across were moving, cracking free, splintering against the dam wall, grinding against its face, and soon thousands of tons of ice would be moving down through the sluices. Rose was on his knees but as Starling and Ben watched, fascinated, horror-struck, the finger slipped blackly towards the crouching man and he lurched, the fissure opened and he was slipping sideways. He cried out once, and then his staring pale face remained looking up to them as he seemed to lean across at a crazy angle, one leg pinned in the fissure. The grinding noise had increased, and the whole mass of ice now seemed to be on the move, pushing remorselessly forward against the face of the dam. The narrow fissure trapping Rose disappeared and the man was on his side, hands on the ice, helpless, twisting; it reopened suddenly with a great rushing and he slipped under, his head and shoulders just visible before the ice ground in again, and Ben turned aside at the one scream, cut off in mid-air.

A few seconds later Grant Starling turned too, and took Ben's arm.

'He's gone,' he said tonelessly, and it was as though for him Edward Rose had never existed.

5

Grant Starling was a hard and determined

man who had fought his way to the top of the construction industry in Canada through sheer hard work, inspiration and grit. During the week after Edward Rose's death he devoted his considerable energies to discovering just what had been going on behind his back in Starling Enterprises, and what had happened in Fairmont Valley seven years previously.

Rider and Ben felt very much as though they were dragged along on the tail of a whirlwind. They were there when Starling verbally beat Seth Davis into a shivering hulk, and they flew across country with him to interview Haggett, the lawyer whom Rose had placed high in one of the Starling companies and who had been hand in glove with Rose in the various fraudulent enterprises that the man had conducted. And as the investigation undertaken by Starling proceeded Ben was also to watch the change in Grant Starling; hard he was still, and as determined as ever, but as the truth unfolded Ben saw an uncertainty creep into the old man's eyes. Grant Starling had viewed himself, all his life, as a man who knew his way in life, who could sum up a man's character, who was unshackled by weakness and emotion, but now he was beginning to realize he had been living in a world of his own imagination. He had surrounded himself with power and delegated much of it to men he trusted, like Edward Rose. He had not suspected betrayal.

The truth about Rose was hard to appreciate but the truth about his son was harder to take. Ben tried to explain it to Pete Henley when he finally returned to England, and the office.

'I had to admire him, for the way he ripped into it in spite of the hurt. His son had been completely under Rose's influence even to the extent of the Fenokee deal, even though he nearly wrecked it by taking Joanna to the lodge. What hurt Grant Starling was the fact that Philip provided some of the hush money by conning his own father into paying off one of the witnesses. That cheque paid Joe Pearl to say the brakes weren't faulty; and Haggett paid Nebbia, and Durrance – who'd got curious as to why Joanna was in the valley at all. Grant Starling aged, Pete, as he heard it all.'

Pete nodded thoughtfully.

'Rose must have thought himself safe as the years went by.'

'Yes. The Project went ahead, the witnesses scattered … but the first cloud appeared with the congressional enquiry into Roberts's activities. It wasn't directed against the Fenokee Project but if it dug too deep the deal could be exposed. He sat tight and hoped and he might still have got away with it … but Joe Pearl died, with a Mormon conscience.'

'When did Rose learn that Pearl's widow had written to you?'

'Only after I visited Nebbia, who wouldn't see me. Nebbia phoned Haggett and Haggett did the checking. Rose wasted no time: once he heard I was visiting Seth Davis he told him that I had to be eliminated. My questions on top of the congressional enquiry were too much. Davis denies it but I think he asked him to take me to the spillway dam and get rid of me. Rose was certainly up there, pressuring him, reminding him that Seth too had been paid for silence, with the spillway project.'

'And Seth Davis agreed.'

'He says not. He says he was torn with conscience and refused but I don't believe him – particularly since he'd cut costs on the dam as well and had that hanging over him. Rose left the dam, then phoned Seth, insisting he get rid of me. In a moment of distress, Seth says, he played for time by depressing the switch. Stranding me in the cage would give him time to think.'

'That's all he did? Strand you?'

'So he says. He argues it was then taken out of his hands when someone else switched on the power again in the control house and the pin sheared. Of course, he didn't realize Frank Carson was suspicious about the whole thing. Anyway, Rose was mad but could do no more since he and Starling were off to England. Things just simmered then until I asked for an interview with Grant Starling. Rose played on the old man's affection for his son and got me thrown out, then told Grant he'd get me off his back by fixing the Cornelius contract. With luck that would settle me; at least it would buy time.'

'You mean he was under pressure from the congressional enquiry?'

'Not only that. Pearl was dead, Nebbia was scared into silence, Seth was too deeply involved to be a threat but Durrance... Sam was realizing there could be more money from the source he'd tapped seven years ago. He contacted Haggett after Rider's visit–'

'And Rose killed him.'

'We can't prove it, but it looks that way. If Nebbia had caused trouble he'd have gone the same way but just then Rose was at his wits' end. New problems were rising at each turn and the final straw was my appearance at the dam when he was already trying to explain to Grant how Seth got the contract and fouled it up with a botched construction system.'

Ben hitched himself forward as Pete's eyebrows went up, in surprise.

'The spillway dam was never adequately costed, Pete, but Seth got the contract as payment for keeping his mouth shut about Philip and Joanna. But when the ice built up and Grant went up there to find out what was happening, in view of the construction techniques Seth had used, trouble was brewing for Rose and Davis.'

'Your arrival meant that Rose had finally lost control of the situation.'

'Ahuh. He guessed he couldn't stop me talking to Starling other than by killing me. So he suggested we go down to the dam wall to watch for the ice breaking. I doubt whether he also wanted to kill Starling but it was forced on him once we started talking. I guess he thought he could stage it as an accident – me falling and Grant Starling trying to save me, both of us mangled by the ice. Instead...'

He was silent and Pete sat staring at him for a moment.

'Anyway, it's all over now, Ben.'

Ben knew what he meant.

'Yes, it's finished.' He looked up suddenly and grinned in a way he hadn't for a long time. 'And there's a lot of work to be done.'

'You're right. I haven't been able to sort out much of the Cornelius smash but–'

'Forget it. Starling's putting it right – we won't get the Hotels Chain but we'll get adequate compensation and Grant will be putting a few extra contracts our way in addition. Not to mention the slice he wants to take in our firm!'

He saw Pete Henley sit up and begin to glow. It was a good sight.

'He wants to come in with us–'

'And finance some of our expansion.'

Pete expressed his delight by slamming one huge hand down on the desk, jumping to his feet and prowling around, lumbering across the room like an over-excited grizzly bear. For several minutes he exclaimed over what they could do with financial backing and then at last he calmed, and faced Ben somewhat hesitantly.

'By the way, we … uh… Harriet was saying this morning that she … uh … bumped into Carol Taylor last week, in town. Invited her over to dinner Saturday. Harriet said this morning that … uh … now you're back home you might care to … uh … make it a foursome.'

In spite of himself Ben's mind was suddenly crowded with images. He remembered the grim line of Grant Starling's mouth as he listened to Haggett outline Rose's and Philip's betrayal of his trust and his face when he stated he'd now be giving evidence at Roberts's congressional enquiry. There was the figure of Edward Rose slipping into grinding ice, raising a last desperate cry; there was the hazy, half-seen image of Philip Starling, the man he'd never known, with Joanna, lonely, unhappy … dying in the snow. There were the drawn blinds at he windows of the Parkland Nursing Home, Graham Nebbia waiting for

the hearing that would destroy his professional career. There was the sad chubby
figure of Billy Pearl waiting at Waterton Park
for the buyer who would take off his hands
the garage his father had bought with blood-
stained money.

And there was Mary Davis.

The whole evil of the world had suddenly
come to her doorstep and no longer had she
been able to hide her face from the brutal
realities that lay outside her domestic state.
She had been happy with Seth, secure and
satisfied in her marriage, asking only careful
questions and none that could produce
dangerous answers, but now the truth had
been forced upon her as Seth faced a term
of imprisonment for his part in the Roberts
affair and Joanna's death. It was Ben who
had had to tell her because he felt
responsible and because Joanna had been
her friend. She had heard him out stonily
and had said nothing, not even goodbye. He
knew they would never meet again, for he
had destroyed her world.

But that was all past now, Mary, Seth,
Joanna, all past, and finished with.

'Ben?'

Pete's tone was uncertain as he broke into
Ben's silence. Ben looked up and smiled.

'Yes, I think I'd like to make it a foursome,
Pete. I'd like it very much.'

The publishers hope that this book has given you enjoyable reading. Large Print Books are especially designed to be as easy to see and hold as possible. If you wish a complete list of our books please ask at your local library or write directly to:

Dales Large Print Books
Magna House, Long Preston,
Skipton, North Yorkshire.
BD23 4ND